The Eclipse of

Moonbeam Dawson

Also by Jean Davies Okimoto

NOVELS

My Mother Is Not Married to My Father
It's Just Too Much
Norman Schnurman, Average Person
Who Did It, Jenny Lake?
Jason's Women
Molly by Any Other Name
Take a Chance, Gramps!
Talent Night
The Eclipse of Moonbeam Dawson

PICTURE BOOKS

Blumpoe the Grumpoe Meets Arnold the Cat
A Place for Grace
No Dear, Not Here

SHORT STORIES

"Jason the Quick and the Brave"
"Moonbeam Dawson and the Killer Bear"
"Next Month . . . Hollywood!"
"Watching Fran"
"Eva and the Mayor"

PLAYS

Hum It Again, Jeremy
Uncle Hideki

NONFICTION, COAUTHOR

Boomerang Kids: How to Live with
Adult Children Who Return Home

The Eclipse of
Moonbeam Dawson

Jean Davies Okimoto

A Tom Doherty Associates Book/New York

THE ECLIPSE OF MOONBEAM DAWSON

Copyright © 1997 by Jean Davies Okimoto

A scene from the novel is based on the story "Moonbeam Dawson and the Killer Bear," which first appeared in *Connections: Short Stories by Outstanding Writers for Young Adults,* edited by Donald R. Gallo, published by Bantam Doubleday Dell, and reprinted in *Features,* published by Nelson Canada, and in *Relating,* published by Prentice Hall Canada, Inc.

This book is printed on acid-free paper.

A Tor Book
Published by Tom Doherty Associates, Inc.
175 Fifth Avenue
New York, NY 10010

Tor Books on the World Wide Web: http://www.tor.com

Tor® is a registered trademark of Tom Doherty Associates, Inc.

Design by Lynn Newmark

Library of Congress Cataloging-in-Publication Data

Okimoto, Jean Davies.
  The eclipse of Moonbeam Dawson / Jean Davies Okimoto.
    p. cm.
  "A Tom Doherty Associates book."
  Summary: Raised on a commune by a granola-munching ex-hippie mother, fifteen-year-old Moonbeam realizes that nothing is normal in his life and so sets out to change things.
  ISBN 0-312-86244-X
  [1. Mothers and sons—Fiction. 2. Interpersonal relations—Fiction.] I. Title.
  PZ7.0415Ec 1997
  [Fic]—dc21   97-19533
                                                   CIP
                                                   AC

First Edition: November 1997

Printed in the United States of America

0 9 8 7 6 5 4 3 2 1

For Nina and Joseph Norman

Acknowledgments

I would like to thank my friends in Seattle and in British Columbia for their help with Moonbeam's story: Katie Ellis, Tami Jones, and Richard Beaupied of Bear Watch, and the real Tom Stere, Gretchen Coe, and Jim Goltz.

The Eclipse of
Moonbeam Dawson

Chapter One

Moonbeam Dawson sat in the old truck watching the rain pound against the windshield. It was getting darker by the minute. The place was giving him the creeps. The ancient trees surrounding the parking lot began to look like monsters with shaggy black arms towering against the steely sky. Weird. It didn't even seem like the same place he'd been with the commune school. That day it had been sunny, and the park glittered a hundred shades of green so beautiful he couldn't believe it. Now he just wanted to get out of here. She better hurry up, he thought. At the rate they were going he wasn't sure they'd ever get anywhere tonight, especially the ferry. That was a joke.

Moonbeam leaned his head back against the seat. Things were going to be different when they got to the gulf islands. Some things were definitely going to change, he promised himself. No matter what she said.

Abby Dawson emerged from the park bathroom, lowered her head to shield her face from the driving rain, and ran to the truck.

"You better go, too." She climbed in on the driver's side.

"You're *telling* me I should go!"

"I'm just suggesting."

"I'm sixteen!"

"Fifteen. You won't be sixteen for three months. I happen to know your birthday. I was there when you were born."

Moonbeam rolled his eyes and stared at the forest in front of them. Sometimes she was really not funny. *I was there when you were born.* Hilarious.

Abby pulled off the hood of her parka, shaking her hair. "It's so phony. It really galls me."

"What?"

"The way they name this part of the park *McMullen* Emerald Forest, as if the greedy scum actually give a fig for these old trees. It's all for the tourists. A quarter of a million supposedly come through here every year. They want them to think Mc-Mullen Blundeel is preserving the forests because of this one bloody park!"

"It's a scam," Moonbeam agreed.

"You're darn right it is." Abby turned the key to start the truck. The engine started to turn over, then whined and didn't catch. She looked nervously at the ignition. "Don't do this to me. Please, not now."

"I told you—"

She glared at Moonbeam. "It probably is the battery and *don't* say it," she threatened, as she pumped the gas and frantically turned the key again. "I don't want to discuss it. Just pray to the Goddess of Car Engines to help us out."

"She's a 'he,' and it's probably the battery so we should pray to Gob, God of Batteries."

"I don't care who it is, just ask for this truck not to die on us." She crossed her fingers, turned off the key, pumped the gas pedal, looked skyward, mumbled something indistinguishable, and tried the ignition again.

"Voila!" she shouted joyfully as the engine turned over. "Thank you, Gob." She grinned at Moonbeam. Triumphantly, she shifted into reverse but had barely gotten it in gear when the engine died. Panicky, she tried it again. Then again and again, each time growing more frantic.

"Mum, don't! You'll flood it!"

"Don't yell at me!" Abby snapped.

She stared straight ahead, then bit her lip and put her head down on the steering wheel.

Moonbeam didn't look at her, not wanting to know whether she was collecting her thoughts or crying. Hopefully not crying. There'd been enough of that last night. Although he had to admit he really couldn't blame her, the way all her dreams went down the toilet yesterday.

"Look, Mum," Moonbeam said quietly. "We don't have a lot of choices here. We're not walking back to Port Alberni or walking on to Parksville, so the best thing is to just wait here and I'll try and flag somebody down."

"Okay," Abby sniffed. Then after a bit, she lifted her head off the wheel and rummaged in her pocket. She pulled out a Kleenex and blew her nose. "Guess it's you and me against the world, eh?" She gave him a brave smile.

"Sure, Mum." Moonbeam turned away from her and rolled down the window so he could look back at the road. She'd said that his whole life and lately it was beginning to make him cringe. But it was no time to argue. He'd spotted headlights. A pair of small yellow dots rounding the corner at the edge of the park. Moonbeam jumped out of the truck and tore across the parking lot, but by the time he reached the highway the car had passed. British Columbia plates, driving pretty fast. Probably a local who knows the roads well. Moonbeam pulled the hood of his parka down lower over his face and decided he better stay by the edge of the road. If the car was going the speed limit, there was no way he could sprint and make it from the truck in time for a driver to see him. Especially in this rain. He stuck his hands in his pockets and waited.

He knew something like this would happen. Leaving Heather Mountain was a big, disorganized mess. She said she wanted to be up and out of there at the crack of dawn. Right. It was midafternoon before they finally left. He should have stayed in bed. Then when he said they ought to have the truck checked out in Port Alberni, she didn't want to. "We're getting such a late start, Moonbeam. It'll just take too much time, the truck will be fine. This old thing has good karma."

Right. Moonbeam glanced back at his mother sitting huddled behind the steering wheel of the old truck. It looked pitiful sitting there in the rain, piled high with all their stuff. It had been tricky packing her loom with bags of rice and beans all around it to protect it, then covering everything with that raggedy brown tarp. The old Toyota pickup was as battered as its faded bumper sticker, ARMS ARE MADE FOR HUGGING, but the words were still readable and the truck still ran, at least until now. So much for the good karma.

She was always talking about stuff like that, karma and omens and the way the planets lined up, and also inventing Goddesses for everything. None of it did her much good. Things just never seemed to turn out very well for her. But he didn't have the heart to tell her he was secretly glad things had fallen apart at Heather Mountain.

Moonbeam stared at the empty highway. Where were all those quarter of a million tourists when they needed them? All those cars with the plates from Alberta, Saskatchewan, Manitoba, Ontario, Quebec, Washington, Oregon, California, and Idaho. Why weren't they here right now, vacationing in British Columbia in this very spot, cruising through Emerald Forest Park?

Amazing how deserted this road was. It was definitely spooky out here. Moonbeam jumped, thinking he heard something on the other side of the road. *Clunk* . . . "What's that?" he whispered aloud, trying to see into the forest. He was sure he heard something in there. Sort of a hollow thumping sound . . . *Clunk* . . . There it was again. Probably just the wind, he told himself. A dead branch banging against a . . . *Clunk* . . . tree or something. Was there actually such a thing as a sasquatch? The huge, hairy, manlike creature with long arms that supposedly lives in the mountain forests on the west coast of North America. He felt a knot tightening in his stomach.

Moonbeam tried to think of something to get his mind off the clunking noise. Think about when the school was here, he told himself. Think about the time line we made about the trees to get an idea of how old they were. He had liked making that time line. It was ... *Clunk* ... cool. Some of the trees were here in A.D. 1215, over 780 years ago, making them two hundred and three hundred years old when Columbus ... *Clunk* ... came to North America ... *Clunk* ... And in the winter of 1535, when Jacques Cartier's ... *Clunk* ... ship was frozen in the ice at the mouth of the St. Charles at Quebec City, some of ... *Clunk* ... the trees were already giants ... *Clunk*.

Moonbeam spotted headlights again, another pair of two small yellow dots. Let's hope this is a good person, he thought. The lights got a little bigger and he forgot about the clunking noise. Actually, a medium person would do, as long as they have jumper cables. But what if? He swallowed hard, feeling his fingers grow numb with fear. What if it was a rotten person? An evil scum. The headlights got larger and he saw the headlines on the *Alberni Valley Times*. On Victoria's *Time Colonist*. On the *Vancouver Sun*. It was a big, big story.

MOTHER AND TEENAGE SON
BUTCHERED BY BAD GUY

Abby Dawson, 35, most recently of the Happy Children of the Good Earth Compound near Heather Mountain, and her son Moonbeam, almost 16, were found chopped up in Emerald Forest Park by Constable David Eyre. "It was a real mess," said Eyre, "especially what was left of the kid." The horrible bad guy is still at large.

The lights loomed larger and larger, and Moonbeam saw an old RV coming slowly toward him through the rain. The camper's probably full of body parts he thought, glancing back toward the truck at Abby.

Abby rolled down the truck window and stuck her arm out, wildly waving it. "Flag it, Moonbeam!"

Moonbeam raised his hand tentatively, half hoping the driver would decide he really didn't mean it, that he was just standing by the side of the road exercising, doing tai chi or something, and would drive right by. But the headlights got large, and Moonbeam stood still, caught in the lights like a deer as the RV slowly turned toward him and drove into the parking lot.

Abby leaped out of the truck and ran over to Moonbeam as the driver rolled down his window.

"Need some help?" A sandy-haired guy who looked about forty stuck his head out the window. Clean-shaven, looked okay, very presentable for a serial killer.

"Got cables? We think it's our battery." Abby looked up at the guy like he was the prince himself who'd just galloped up on a white horse.

"Sure, let's see what we can do."

He drove across the lot and pulled in next to the truck while Abby and Moonbeam walked back to meet him.

"I'm Harvey Hattenbach." He held out his hand.

"Abby Dawson."

Watch out, you might be shaking the hand of a serial killer.

"And this is my son, Moonbeam."

Not one word about my name, slime bucket.

"Hi." Moonbeam clenched his teeth as he shook the guy's hand, trying not to imagine it dripping with blood.

Harvey grabbed the handle of the back door of the RV. "Got my cables in here, if I can find them in this mess." He grinned and climbed in the RV. "Say, want a cuppa tea? You both look soaked."

"Sounds good." Abby smiled sweetly. "What do you think, Moonbeam?"

"We don't have time. After we get the jump, the battery's got to get charged and it'll take a couple of hours." Moonbeam picked up a stone and threw it in frustration, wishing he didn't always have to be the one to figure everything out.

"Think we should go back to Port Alberni?"

"Of course." He pulled the hood of his parka down lower over his forehead. "We can camp at China Creek and get the ferry. *First thing* tomorrow."

"We'll be up at the crack of dawn," Abby said earnestly.

"Yeah, right." Moonbeam lifted the hood of the truck and

Harvey attached the cables to their battery. "Get in so you can try it, Mum."

The engine turned over on the third try and Moonbeam took the cables off and handed them to Harvey. "Thanks a lot."

Abby rolled down the window. "I can't tell you how much I appreciate this." She looked up at him, her gray-green eyes sparkling and her voice low and sweet.

"I'll follow you to Port, just in case you have any more problems." He leaned close to the window.

"I'm sure we'll be fine." Moonbeam buckled his seat belt.

"That's really nice of you!" Abby smiled, surprised. "Are you sure?"

"No problem. There's the McDonald's next to the station. I'm about ready for a bite anyway."

Maybe he's a vampire. Moonbeam scowled, folded his arms over his chest, and slumped in the seat.

"See you soon!" Abby waved and backed out of the lot, then waited to get on the highway until Harvey pulled up behind her. "This is so nice of him," she said, looking back in the rearview mirror, her voice gushing with gratitude.

"A lot of people would help out, Mum."

Okay, so he wasn't a serial killer, but we're not talking some kind of hero here. Moonbeam sighed as she pulled out on the highway. Here they were, going backwards! But as he thought about it, he realized they'd only be delayed a day. Knowing the way she went about things, it could have been a lot worse, he decided. A lot worse.

He hadn't hated their life on Heather Mountain. It was better than the crummy apartment they had in Victoria, where people banged on the cheesy walls and you could hear people yelling and TVs blaring. But more and more life in the great outdoors was too small for him. Just like their cabin. She thought it was fine for the two of them, but a couple of years ago Moonbeam felt cramped. He wanted more privacy. (There had one been too many *"Oops!* Sorry, Moonbeam!"s as she barged in on him.) So he and his friend Meadow MacLaine, who was a good carpenter, built a separate space behind the stove. There was no way it could ever be called a room of his own; the space was tiny, more like a berth on a train. But it had the essential architectural feature: a wall between him and his mother.

The other thing that was too small was the group of people. There weren't enough kids and a lot of them were younger. There weren't enough girls, to be specific. The Happy Children of the Good Earth commune had a drastic shortage of girls his age. The only one even close to his age was Starlight Lewis, and it was embarrassing to call twelve close. So this past year Moonbeam and Meadow, who felt the same way, took every chance they got to go into Port Alberni, a town of 20,000, the nearest place of any size. Usually almost every week someone from the commune had to go in for something. Getting teeth fixed, tires patched, and truck parts seemed to be the more common reasons. Moonbeam and Meadow would hang around the video store or McDonald's, or go to the cafe where they had a TV over the lunch counter and watch whatever was on. Didn't matter what. Although the main reason they left Heather Mountain every chance they had wasn't to look at TV. It was to see girls.

Abby pulled into the station at the corner of Redford Road and the Port Alberni Highway, and Harvey drove up next to her.

"I'll meet you at McDonald's." He pointed across the road.

Abby rolled down the window. "I can't thank you enough," she gushed. "We'll be there in a few minutes." She waved as he pulled out of the station.

The gas station guy had them pull the truck into the garage and told them to come back in about an hour.

"This is working out great. It should be ready just about the time we're through eating." Abby smiled as they walked over to McDonald's.

Harvey was sitting at a table by the back windows. Abby waved to him, then read the menu over the counter. While she was looking up, Moonbeam was looking around, scanning the place the way he always did when he came here from Heather Mountain. He had gotten very good at knowing where girls hung out, and this McDonald's was one of the prime locations. Moonbeam spotted a table of girls about his age. Good, at least there'd be some decent scenery. Fine looking girls. No, he definitely would not mind living in Port Alberni, he thought as his eyes darted over the girls. Although he didn't dwell on the idea for more than a split second, because there'd never really be a chance of him living here. His mother. She'd hate it. She always complained about the stench of the paper mill and the big black cloud that would billow from its smokestack.

Abby got a large salad, soup, a roll, and coffee.

"I'll have a Big Mac." Moonbeam put in his order, bracing himself.

"Meat!" His mother hissed through clenched teeth.

"It's *my* stomach." He hissed back at her. He'd been eating meat whenever he left Heather Mountain. It was about time she knew.

"I can't believe you ordered that." Abby glared at his tray. "What about the cow's stomach?"

"So, what about the fish's stomach? You eat fish sometimes." Moonbeam looked at the girls out of the corner of his eye as they passed their table.

"We'll talk about this later," she said in a low voice as they got to Harvey's table. Then she smiled at the guy and slid into the seat across from him. "Thanks again for your help. Things are sure looking better," she said, taking her salad off her tray. "The rain's even let up."

Moonbeam sat next to Harvey where he had the best view of the table of girls.

"Glad I came by. Where you heading?"

"Maybe the Gulf Islands," Abby told him.

"Definitely the Gulf Islands." Moonbeam took a big bite of the hamburger. Abby clenched her teeth and wouldn't look at him. "The only thing we're not sure about is which one."

"You from around here?" Harvey sipped his coffee.

"We lived on Heather Mountain for the last five years." She took a bite of her salad. "Before that, Victoria for a while, before that, Heather Mountain."

"Heather Mountain? Not much up there."

"It was a commune."

"Didn't work out, eh?"

"They took a vow of nonviolence and said the place was a nuclear free zone," Moonbeam explained. "But then there was this big fight and some people started bashing each other with shovels."

"The land was owned by a man who inherited it from his father. He told everyone to clear out." Abby looked sad. "The first time we lived off the land like that, the weather got us. The crops froze and we couldn't make it. But I never thought it would end because the people couldn't get along." Abby stared out the window for a moment, lost in thought.

Moonbeam gazed at the girls, wondering what it would be like to go to school with a bunch of them like that.

Abby sighed, then looked at Harvey. "What about you? Where you from?"

Moonbeam chewed slowly, trying to enjoy each bite. Meat tasted better when his mother wasn't sitting right there clenching her teeth. Then he looked over at the girls again. The one with the curly brown hair was really fine.

"Toronto originally. But I got sick of the rat race. Been in Tofino the past two years."

Abby nodded. "I don't think I could go back to a city. I'm from Seattle originally."

Weird. She hardly ever tells anybody she's from the states. Moonbeam looked at the girls. The one at the end with the blue sweatshirt was really something.

"Yankee, eh?"

"I just claim Canadian now. You used to be able to have dual citizenship even if you weren't born in Canada, if one parent was Canadian. My father's American, my mother was from Vancouver."

"Been up here long?"

"Since college."

What is he, a reporter or something? What a nosy guy. Moonbeam sipped his Coke. The one in the middle in the tight sweater wasn't bad either.

"What do you do in Tofino?" she asked.

"I'm with the Clayoquot Biosphere Project."

"Part of Friends of Clayoquot Sound?" Abby broke off a little piece of the roll and popped it in her mouth. "We were there in ninety-three for the protests."

"The biosphere project's strictly scientific. But I was in the protests in ninety-three. Most everyone in town was."

Abby smiled at him. "Maybe we already met, but didn't remember."

"No." He smiled, leaning across the table. "I wouldn't have forgotten if I met you."

Abby laughed, flattered.

"I was there, too." Moonbeam piped up, then took another big bite, chewing noisily. "Only they didn't arrest me, just Mum."

"Actually, I was considering heading to the coast to Tofino, but I thought we'd have a better chance of finding work in the Gulf Islands. I want to work outdoors, but we'll take whatever we can get."

"There's a new lodge opening on Stere Island."

"Where's that?" Abby seemed interested.

"We're going to the Gulf Islands, Mum," Moonbeam reminded her.

"It's west of Tofino. The land's being leased from the Clayoquot band. It's part of the Nuu-chah-nulth efforts to develop economically. I think indigenous people get priority in hiring, but the jobs are open to non Native people, too."

"Moonbeam might get priority. He's half Haida."

Fine. Just tell him our whole life story why don't you? And NOT ONE WORD about my name, buddy. Moonbeam looked over at the girls. The first thing he was going to do when they got to the gulf islands was change his name. He'd been thinking about it for a long time and now that they were leaving

Heather Mountain it was the perfect time to do it. He'd have some good regular name, so when he met girls his age at least he wouldn't have that to worry about.

"It's a really posh place," Harvey continued. "Caters to rich tourists. I'm pretty sure they're hiring now." He took a last sip of his coffee. "Well, got to get on my way."

Harvey stood up and hesitated by the table. "Look me up if you ever get to Tofino. I'm the only Harvey Hattenbach."

"Thanks. And thanks again for everything." Abby smiled, then glared at Moonbeam, kicking him under the table.

"Yeah, thanks," Moonbeam muttered.

"And if you want to check out that new lodge, let me know. The manager's a friend of mine."

"Great. Thanks." Abby looked up at him, smiling gratefully. "I can't tell you how much I appreciate this, Harvey," she said softly.

Oh yuk, gag. Just leave, buddy.

Abby watched him as he walked across the restaurant and out the door. She grinned and gave a thumbs-up to Harvey as he waved to them from the parking lot.

"Guess we better go, too, eh?" Abby sighed, then crunched up her napkin and put it on her tray. "Ready?"

"I've been ready for the past fifteen minutes. You're the one that kept talking to that guy."

"He was very nice."

"The sun's going down. It's going to be a hassle getting the tent up."

"We've put it up before in the dark."

"Yeah. And it's a hassle."

Moonbeam stood up and glanced at the group of girls. He wished he could get up the nerve to smile at one of them as they walked by their table. But instead he just looked at the floor. This is going to change, he told himself. When they got to the Gulf Islands, he wouldn't have to look at the floor. He'd have his new name and he'd get a lot of practice talking to girls. It would be great.

At the gas station, Abby and Moonbeam got the truck and it started without a hitch. As they headed out on the Alberni Highway, Moonbeam began to think seriously about what he wanted his new name to be. He wanted something regular, maybe like Bob, Bill, John, Tom, Jim, or Tim. He'd have to try out each one. Maybe write them down and pick the best.

Abby started to hum. Whenever they drove any distance, she either sang or hummed the same melody. It was "Peace Train," a tune which she considered her exclusive road trip theme song. Usually after about five miles of "Peace Train" Moonbeam was ready to throw himself screaming from the truck and hitchhike. He liked to imagine the wonderful people who would pick him up. People who didn't sing "Peace Train." People with beautiful daughters his age.

The sun was setting by the time they reached China Creek Park. Moonbeam carried the tent to a campsite. "If we'd gotten an early start and the battery checked, we'd be on the ferry now," he grumbled.

"Not necessarily." Abby helped him lay out the tent. "If the battery died on the back road out of Heather Mountain we might have still been there."

"Maybe." He was too tired to argue. She always had an answer for everything. Whatever his mother did, even if it turned out to be totally dumb, she always had some reason why it was okay. Not an excuse, but a reason.

Moonbeam pounded in the last stake, then got their sleeping bags out of the truck.

"I'm glad this park's got a shower. I'll wash this mess in the morning." Abby pulled off the woven scrunchy that held back her hair and ran her hands through the long, brownish-blond strands. "Too tired tonight." She turned up the collar of her flannel shirt and crawled in her sleeping bag, pulling it tight around her. "Night, honey."

"Night, Mum." Moonbeam got in his bag and lay there, looking up at the roof of the tent. It definitely was sagging a bit. He hoped the stupid thing didn't collapse.

His mother started snoring. She was out all right. He edged down in his sleeping bag, but it was a chilly night and he couldn't get warm. Better go to the truck and get a sweatshirt.

Moonbeam stood over the truck bed and dug through his backpack. Yanking out his sweatshirt, he put his arms in the sleeves and lifted it to pull it over his head, then stopped for a minute to look up at the sky. The stars were brilliant. *Up above the world so high, like a diamond in the sky.* He remembered singing with the little kids the night they all lay in the field on Heather Mountain learning about the planets, huddled together in a heap, like puppies.

He pulled on his sweatshirt and looked across at their tent. It looked so small sitting there alone in the campground dwarfed by the mammoth trees. He rubbed his hands together and blew on them to get warm, then went back to the tent.

Opening the flap, he saw that his mother was sleeping soundly. He took one last look at the stars. He could see Orion's belt and opposite the handle in the bowl of the Big Dipper the pointer stars were shining clearly, pointing the way to Polaris, the north star. Moonbeam stood outside the tent for a minute, wondering which one of the Gulf Islands he'd be living on the next time he looked up at the stars.

Chapter Two

"Oh, rats." Abby propped herself up in her sleeping bag as she heard rain against the tent. She listened to its steady drumming for a minute, then sighed and glanced over at the lanky heap in the sleeping bag next to her, now visible as the gray light of dawn seeped under the front flap. Moonbeam slept quietly, facing the wall of the tent with his back toward her. Only the top of his head protruded from the blue nylon cocoon.

"Moonbeam." She poked his shoulder.

Silence.

"*Moon*beam." She poked harder.

"Mmrggh."

"Moonbeam, it's raining." More poking.

"Gghrmp." He grunted, batting her arm away like a pesky mosquito.

Abby grabbed her gumboots and banged them together over the top of his head.

"What the . . ." He opened his eyes, startled to see the black rubber boots hanging over him, inches from his nose. He swatted them away, sat up, and glowered at her.

"Your alarm clock." She smiled sweetly, dangling the boots.

"Couldn't you sing or something?"

"It's raining." Abby wiggled out of her sleeping bag and began pulling on her boots.

"So?"

"So, what do you think we should do?"

"Well," he snarled, "I don't think we can stop the rain, Mum."

"Don't be sarcastic. What I mean is, should we pack up and leave now, or wait a bit and see if it stops?"

"We could wait here all day for it to stop!"

"I didn't say all day, I said just wait a bit."

Abby looked away and bit her lower lip. He hated it when she did that, it was usually when he'd hurt her feelings and she'd just clam up. Go silent on him. All quiet, like her body was still there but she'd left. Her silence was a pain. Better to have her bark at him. Moonbeam pulled his legs out of the sleeping bag.

"Okay," she said quietly. "We'll get going."

"And we need to decide which of the Gulf Islands we're trying first. We have to know that by the time we get to the ferry."

"Moonbeam, I've been thinking—"

"I'll get the map." Moonbeam pulled on his boots and left the tent. He didn't want any more delays. It was time to get on with it. He brought the map of Vancouver Island back to the tent and spread it out on the floor at the foot of their sleeping bags.

"Still really coming down, eh?"

Moonbeam took off his parka and tossed it in the corner of the tent. "Yeah, probably take a bit of work to get a fire going."

He sat next to her, crossing his long legs. "Okay, we're here. China Creek Park." He pointed to a tan circle on the map on the east side of Alberni Inlet.

"Moonbeam, I've been thinking. Maybe the Gulf Islands aren't such a great idea."

"We already decided!"

"Don't yell. I'm just thinking it over."

"Okay, let's think it over." Moonbeam thought about the girls in McDonald's. "How 'bout somewhere closer to Port Alberni, where there are more jobs."

"I'm not living in Port Alberni," she said defiantly.

Moonbeam threw his head back, rolling his eyes. "I didn't say for us to *live* there. I just said—"

"Okay, okay. All I'm saying is that we should try resort areas first."

"You said all that before."

"I'm just thinking about it again. Tourism is the biggest industry on Vancouver Island."

"Next to logging."

"Don't remind me. Okay, second biggest. Therefore, our chances are best if we think resorts."

"That's what we decided." Moonbeam rolled his eyes, totally exasperated.

"Like I realized yesterday, I'd only consider cooking for loggers as a last resort." Abby paused and stared at him. "Well?"

"Well, what?"

"Aren't you going to laugh at my little joke. Last resort, get it?"

"Heh-heh."

"Okay, so don't indulge me." Abby looked at the map. "See if I'll ever laugh again at any of your dumb jokes. Anyway, I think rather than the Gulf Islands we should try Tofino."

"Tofino! It takes forever to get to Victoria or Vancouver from there!"

"It was an omen, Moonbeam."

"Oh, jeez. You mean that guy, Harry."

"Harvey. His name's Harvey."

"I don't care what his name is!"

"I think we're supposed to go to Tofino. His friend is the manager of that new resort and they're hiring. How do we know the jobs aren't all taken in the Gulf Islands?"

"We won't know anything until we go there and find out. What if the resort in Tofino doesn't hire us?" Moonbeam glared at her. "What about that?"

"There's other places there. Bed and breakfasts and marinas and a bunch of restaurants. People have to eat."

"Yeah. Well, I'm hungry."

Abby stared at the map. "We'll head to back to Port Alberni, then down to Tofino."

"I'm very hungry."

"We can camp at Pacific Rim Park and then call Harvey and he can—"

"I'M STARVING!"

"Well you don't have to scream at me." She folded up the map and dug through her backpack. "Here." She pulled out a couple of apples and handed one to him. "This should take the edge off until we get to Port Alberni. We can get something at the McDonald's and then head to Tofino."

When they got to McDonald's, Moonbeam grabbed the *Alberni Valley Times* from the rack next to the cash register. He was glad they were inside where it was warm; they were still damp from taking down the tent and loading it on the truck. They got their food and found a table.

"First a cow, now a pig." Abby munched on her cinnamon roll, looking at him with disapproval.

Moonbeam peered over the paper. "It's a sausage McMuffin with an egg and it's *my* stomach."

"But who's paying for it?"

Moonbeam buried his head behind the paper, ignoring her. *When I'm on my own I won't have to put up with this garbage. But what if I could get a job? Really live on my own.* Not have to go where *she* decided for once.

He ran his finger down the Help Wanted column: Auto body repairman, Child welfare social worker position, Hair stylist apprentice, Lose all weight be paid, Part-time janitor, Baby-sitter my home, Manager trainee, Shipper/receiver, Taxi driver, Shake block cutter, Wtd: mature couple to be live-in mngrs for 37 suite apt. complex. *Mature couple.* Wonder what they meant by mature? *Lose all weight be paid.* Pretty weird. Wouldn't a person be dead if they lost all weight? Who'd pay for that? he wondered.

"I hope we can make it." A hint of worry crept into her voice. She looked out the window and took a sip of her coffee.

Moonbeam put the paper down. "We've got"—he munched on his McMuffin—"plenty of gas."

"Don't talk with your mouth full."

He glared at her and wiped his mouth. "Then why start up a conversation as soon as I take a bite?"

"Forget it. The Queen's not here." She winked at him.

Moonbeam couldn't help laughing. It was an old joke between them, gauging their behavior by whether or not the Queen of England was on the premises or about to make an appearance. *Better wash your hands in case the Queen comes. Change your shirt, Her Majesty might be arriving. You look smashing, the Queen will approve.*

Abby's smile began to fade and she turned to look out the window again. "I was thinking about money, when I said I hope we can make it."

"Oh, that."

"Yeah, that." She sipped the last of her coffee. "We'll have to pay rent. Which of course we didn't have to do all the years we were on Heather Mountain, but the money my mother left me helps a bit. I wish what I make from weaving was steady enough."

"If wishes were horses."

"Right, I'd be a rich lady."

"Don't forget. I'll be getting a job, too."

She nodded. "I know. I'm counting on both of us." Abby crumpled up her napkin and grabbed her jacket. "Okay, let's go for it. On to Tofino!"

Unless some other omen comes along and she decides she's supposed to live in Parksville and sell Nanaimo bars at a roadside stand. Moonbeam fumed as they walked to the truck. Not because he was that upset about going to Tofino. Where they ended up wasn't as important as what was there. Girls, and kids his own age. And Tofino was cool. He really liked it when they were there in ninety-three. True, it wasn't as close to Vancouver as the Gulf Islands, but it would have a lot more people his age than Heather Mountain. A lot more girls, for sure. Almost any town would. No. The thing that got to him was the way the whole thing came down. Once she figured that guy from Tofino was an omen, any protest Moonbeam made would have been like spitting in the wind.

"Now I've been happy lately . . . thinking about the good things to come . . ." Abby began to sing the minute they got back in the truck. Maybe someone would come and decide his mother was nuts and put him in a foster home. A nice foster home where the people had a few daughters. Maybe one who was eighteen, an older, experienced daughter who was extremely beautiful and would sneak into his room at night.

". . . cause out of the edge of darkness . . . there rides a peace train . . ."

And he would have his new name at the nice foster home. Tim, or maybe Tom. Tom Dawson. Yes. A definite possibility. And the beautiful daughter was Andrea.

"Oh Tom," the beautiful daughter Andrea would say, "we are so thrilled you have come to live here. Isn't it wonderful that my room is right next to yours!" Andrea would smile and gaze at him with her sparkly blue eyes, tossing her thick blond hair as she spoke. She would also stand quite near to him and brush up against him.

Then, after they had a fantastic dinner out at a nice restaurant, like Smitty's or a cafeteria-type place where they gave you all you could eat for $8.95, the happy foster family would go home to their cozy cabin in the woods. They would sit around watching TV and eating popcorn. Then, the nice foster parents would go to bed.

"Goodnight, Tom," the foster mother would say. "Sleep well. Sleep as late as you can in the morning."

"Yes, Tom," the nice foster father would say, "just sleep in and get rest. Take it easy. We don't need you to do any work around here. Having your company is what we care about. Now I have someone to watch Hockey Night in Canada with."

"Yes," says the nice mother, "we have always wanted a son."

"The missus is right," says the father, "a son just like you, Tom."

Then the foster parents go to bed. Then Andrea whispers goodnight and gives Tom a little kiss.

Tom goes into his bedroom and gets in some nice pajamas they bought him at Sears. The pajama shirt is identical to a Canuck's jersey. The parents in this nice foster home can afford to buy such nice pajamas for their new son, Tom. The son they have always wanted.

Tom climbs into bed. It is not a sleeping bag, but real sheets and a nice soft blanket. Also from Sears. The very best they have. The sheets are very clean and soft and Tom snuggles down under the covers. Tom closes his eyes and begins to drift off to sleep, warm and cozy in his new home.

Tap . . . tap . . . tap.

Tom stirs in his sleep, not quite sure if he heard a little tapping sound or if it is part of a dream.

Tap . . . tap . . . tap.

Tom opens his eyes. *Tap . . . tap . . . tap.* There it is again. He is sure now. Someone is knocking at the door.

"Tom?" Andrea whispers. "Tom, it's me, Andrea."

Tom stretches slowly like a giant cat, his muscles rippling under the Canuck's pajama top, then, springing like a cougar, he leaps to the door and opens it.

Andrea throws herself into his arms. "Oh, Tom, I have waited for this moment from the minute you came to live with us."

Silently, Tom closes the door behind them and pulls her into his bedroom. Andrea drops her robe, her blond hair shimmers against her creamy skin, and the moonlight streams through the window, filtering through the trees, and lets Tom get a good look. Wow.

"Shhh, we must not wake my parents," whispers Andrea.

"Of course not," Tom whispers as Andrea takes his hand and pulls him toward the bed.

Moonbeam closed his eyes and smiled as Andrea, older, ex-perienced, beautiful Andrea romped with Tom in Tom's room in the nice foster home. Tom did not have to worry about mess-

ing up because older, experienced Andrea knew all about everything. They did it almost all the way to Tofino.

"Isn't that something?" Abby smiled as they passed the
Kennedy Lake road.

"What is?"

"That we were both here at the Peace Camp in ninety-
three."

"Hfmg," Moonbeam grunted.

"You've sure been quiet."

"Just sleepy."

"Well, I think it's something that he was here and we were,
too."

"That guy Harry?"

"Harvey. Why can't you get it right? His name is Harvey."

"So what if he was here? A lot of people were here." Moonbeam looked at what was called the Black Hole, the old clear-
cut that had housed the village of protesters. "Twelve thousand.
Remember?"

"Of course, I remember."

"Man, it's really coming down." Moonbeam was hoping
there'd be a break in the storm by the time they reached the
campground. They were pretty close. He could smell the ocean
as they took the highway through Pacific Rim Park, and when
they drove along Long Beach, he got his first glimpse of the
huge, steel gray swells and boiling whitecaps pounding the
beach. Salt spray exploded off the rocks, and next to the road
strong gusts coming off the sea bent the immense branches of
the trees.

"There's probably a pay phone in one of the parking lots,"
Abby said as she turned into the campground at Long Beach.
"I'm going to call him."

"You're sure not wasting any time."

"The early bird gets the worm, Moonbeam. Who knows
how fast they'll fill those jobs at that new lodge." Abby spotted a pay phone at the end of the parking lot next to the bath-

rooms. "I'll be right back." She jumped out of the truck and ran through the rain to the phone booth.

In a second she was back. She climbed in the truck, grinning. "He asked us to his place for dinner. Isn't that great!"

"Depends on the food, I guess."

"What's wrong with you? We should thank our lucky stars Harvey came along when he did yesterday."

"Is he going to call his friend about the jobs?"

"I'm sure he will." Abby started the truck. "We'll eat at his place and by then maybe the storm will have passed and it will be easier to set up camp."

"We've set it up before in the rain."

Abby drove out of the campground onto the highway. "I'm not looking a gift horse in the mouth, Moonbeam. And neither should you."

"You don't even know this guy."

"His name is Harvey. He was in the phone book just like he said."

"So what. Maybe he was just trying to impress you. Maybe he doesn't know the manager of anything."

"Look. If it doesn't work out, we'll look for work at the other resorts around here. Have a little faith, Moonbeam." Abby drove slowly on the highway, looking for roads that led in toward the ocean. "He said it was just a few minutes from here. Past Radar Hill. Oh, there's the road. That must be it." She turned left on a dirt road and they bumped along until they reached a clearing. A stunning shake house stood on the bluff facing the ocean.

"I can't believe this is it." Abby's eyes grew wide.

"There's his RV." Moonbeam tried not to seem surprised. "It has to be."

Abby pulled up to the house just as Harvey came out to meet them. A large German shepherd burst out of the door, dancing around and wagging its tail.

"This is Gretta." Harvey rubbed the dogs ears. "She can get a little too friendly."

"We love dogs." Abby let Gretta sniff her hand and then crouched and patted her. "You've sure got quite a place here."

"Can't see much in this rain. But it faces Kathryn Bay. There's a great beach."

At least he's got a nice dog, Moonbeam thought as he stood next to Abby and patted Gretta. But this place looks like something in the movies. Who is this guy?

"How long have you been here?" Abby asked as she walked by Harvey's side toward the house.

"Two years. But it was being built while I was still in Toronto."

He hired people. Not her style at all. Moonbeam followed Abby and Harvey into the house. There was a room off the kitchen by the back door where Harvey said they could hang their wet coats and leave their boots. Harvey went back outside for a minute, throwing a stick for Gretta.

"Did you hear that?" Moonbeam pulled off his boots.

"What?"

"He didn't even build this house himself."

"So?" Abby looked at her reflection in the window and fluffed up her hair.

After a few minutes, Harvey came in with Gretta on his heels. "I've got some salmon chowder left over from last night. We can warm that up, if that's okay."

"Great. I'll set the table, eh?" She smiled and went to the kitchen with him.

Moonbeam hung up his coat and noticed all the shiny new tools the guy had, all hanging neatly on a corkboard opposite the coat hooks. Then he saw something on a shelf above the coats. Now *that* was really not her style. A gun. Some kind of rifle. For a split second he felt scared, wondering if this guy really could be some kind of rich weirdo. Toronto had a lot of weirdos.

Moonbeam looked out at the rain. Calm down, he told himself. He was probably just a guy who went hunting, and as far as his mother was concerned that would do it right there. She had a real thing about guns. Hated them. All guns. In her

book they were all evil and she usually couldn't stand the people who owned them. As soon as she heard about this, the guy
would be history.

His mother was usually very picky about men. Picky, picky,
picky. In fact, Moonbeam wasn't even sure she liked them too
much. There were a few single men at the Happy Children, but
they were like her brothers. She hadn't been really involved with
anyone since they lived in Victoria, when Gregory Thomas was
always hanging around. He came to town on business and
stayed at the Empress Hotel where she worked.

Gregory Thomas was in the picture for a couple of years,
but Moonbeam never had that much to do with him. Mostly
he just remembered having that stupid baby-sitter, Fiona
whatever-her-name-was. She lived in the apartment down the
hall and he'd have to spend the night at her place when his
mother went out. "Fiona might as well sleep in her own bed
since we'll be out so late," was what she always said. Gregory
Thomas had been no particular loss to Moonbeam, but after
his mother stopped seeing the guy, she seemed to be pretty
down on men.

But this guy, this Harvey guy, was definitely all wrong. They
should be settled at Long Beach now, with their camp all set
up. They would be cooking a nice piece of salmon on a plank
over the fire by now, not about to eat this jerk's leftovers. She
must be really losing it.

The kitchen opened up on a large living room, which had
a round cherry wood table near the kitchen. The whole expanse
looked out on the ocean. Abby was setting the table, as Moonbeam came in the room. There was a fire crackling in the fireplace and next to that he noticed something else she couldn't
stand: a TV.

"Maybe you'd like to watch TV after dinner, Mum?" he
said, smugly pointing it out.

Abby ignored him and went to the kitchen. She tossed the
salad and brought the bowl back to the table.

"Soup's on." Harvey carried in a large pot of smoked
salmon chowder.

Moonbeam had to admit that it was good. But the way his mother went on and on about the dinner, a person would think the guy was the head chef at the Empress. This whole thing was getting to be too much. Moonbeam ate in silence. Slurping up the chowder, chomping on salad and garlic bread, and staring out at the ocean, hoping the storm would end so they might still have a chance of leaving.

"Did you hear that, Moonbeam?"

"What?"

"Harvey called his friend at the new resort and he wants to see us tomorrow."

"That's good." The sooner the better.

"I'm a little worried about a resort, I have to admit." Abby put down her soup spoon. "Ever since I came to Canada I've been trying to get away from the kind of people who go to places like that."

"You have to have money to go there, that's for sure."

As if you're just a regular basic, down-to-earth, back-to-the-land guy. "You have a computer, too, I bet." Moonbeam looked at Harvey.

"In my office." Harvey nodded.

See, a techno-wizard. Just what you hate. Moonbeam gave Abby a knowing glance and took a large bite of garlic bread.

"We were talking about the resort." She scowled at him. "Anyway, it's not that I dislike all people with money, I mean, I'm not that narrow. But there's some who just develop this attitude. It's a smug superiority and I can smell it a mile away. I grew up with it."

Harvey picked up the salad bowl. "Anybody want more?"

"No, thanks." Abby smiled.

"Not really." But go ahead. Pig everything. Moonbeam looked out at the ocean.

Harvey helped himself to more salad. "My family was pretty middle class. My Dad worked in collections at the Toronto Dominion, as an administrative clerk. Very conservative, cautious, saved his money, very careful. He and Mum dreamed of buying an RV and traveling across Canada and the states when he retired. That's all they'd talk about."

"Did they get to do it?" Abby took another ladle of chowder. "More? Moonbeam?"

"Yeah, okay. I'll get my own." Don't need you to spoon it out for me.

"No. And it was a real lesson to me. Probably the major factor in my decision to sell my software company and move out here. He had a heart attack three weeks after he retired." Harvey went to the kitchen and came back with the coffee pot. "Ready?"

"Thanks." Abby held out her cup.

"What about your folks?"

"My dad's a vice-president at Boeing and travels all the time. I never remember him being home for more than about a month." Abby put sugar in her coffee. "I was closest to my mother, but she died of breast cancer when I was fifteen. So my dad had me board at Annie Wright, a private school near Tacoma. I saw him on school holidays. Then he remarried my senior year and sold the house I grew up in. He and my stepmother moved to a suburb on the east side of Lake Washington, Bellevue, which I thought was dreadful." Abby looked thoughtful as she stirred her coffee. "I'm sure I went to the University of British Columbia to feel closer to my mother."

"Can I feed the dog?" Moonbeam held out a crust of garlic bread.

"Sure." Harvey smiled. "But you'll never be able to get rid of her."

Yes I will because we're leaving tonight and I'm not coming back, jerk.

"Here, Gretta!" Moonbeam called the dog, holding out the bread for her.

Harvey looked out at the storm. "It hasn't let up at all. I've got plenty of room. You might as well stay here tonight."

"This is so nice of you!" Abby smiled. "Really? Are you sure?"

"It's no trouble."

"I have to admit, it would be a pain trying to get the tent up tonight." Her voice was warm with appreciation.

"We're not wimps. We could do it." Moonbeam looked out at the rain. "We've done it in worse weather."

"Moonbeam, we'd be crazy to pass up an offer of a warm bed." Abby laughed.

Crazy? Here's what's crazy. You've known this dude for all of five hours and now we're spending the night!

Chapter Three

The closer this island is to town, the better, Moonbeam thought as he and Abby left Harvey's for Tofino. The town was located halfway up the west coast of Vancouver Island, where the Trans Canada Highway came to a halt. Northwest of Tofino, the coast was sparsely populated with occasional homesteaders and Native reserves only reached by boat. The last thing Moonbeam wanted was to be stuck out in the middle of nowhere again.

"Are you sure he said ten?" Moonbeam asked.

"Yes."

He didn't quite believe her. He never quite trusted that she got things right. "Ten o'clock at the Fourth Street dock, you're sure?"

"Yes." She frowned at him. "I'm sure."

"Well, we better get down there."

It was a gray and misty morning with both Lone Cone and Mount Colnett, the highest points on Meares Island, completely covered by thick banks of clouds. As they walked down to the dock, a whale-watching zodiac filled with tourists outfitted in cherry red life suits made its way slowly through the mist in pursuit of the gray whales who migrated in March and April from Baja to Alaska. Moonbeam chuckled to himself, imagining the whales organizing an expedition to swim through

Tofino inlet to watch the people puffed up in the bright red suits. He could see a bunch of whales with cameras hanging out next to a little stand on the ocean floor: THE NEXT WEIRD PEOPLE–WATCHING TOUR LEAVES AT 2:00 P.M.

"Are you absolutely sure he's supposed to meet us here? Not at the First Street dock?"

"I'm sure!" She waited by the Wild Side Charters and Day Break Charters, two sport fishing boats. "Harvey said everyone's on island time."

Either that or she got everything mixed up, he thought as he wandered along the dock reading the names of the boats. *Ocean Drifter, Wanderer II, Ranu, Skipjack, Merilda II, Aranui, Me'ynsa Rae, Shirley Barbara II, Hamish I, Ocean Brave.* There seemed to be a few Native names, maybe fisherman from the Opitsat village across from Tofino. Moonbeam wondered about what Harvey had told them about this resort being leased from the Clayoquot band, about their giving priority in hiring to Native people. It seemed kind of phony to use that since he never knew his father. Just his name, Daniel Dawson, and that he was a Haida, and a little bit about how she met him. She never talked about him much.

Growing up on the Happy Children of the Good Earth commune and then those few years in Victoria, most everyone in Moonbeam's world was white, like his mother. He'd never even been on a reserve, and the only Indians he knew were a few kids at King Edward in grade two, and their grandparents had come from Bombay, east Indians from India, not first nation indigenous people. Sure, he knew a lot of the Native legends from the commune school; they were big on that stuff. But he had no actual connection with Native people other than his blood.

He wasn't sure if he even looked part Native. He did have dark, straight hair and dark eyes, and his shoulders were broad, but his features were sort of a hodge-podge and it seemed to him that as far as his looks went, his roots could have been just about anywhere except Scandinavia or Africa. He found the whole thing pretty confusing, to say the least.

He glanced at a Department of Fisheries and Oceans sign, NO DRESSING FISH ON DOCK, and chuckled again. Maybe it was because he had been raised with no TV, but he was always seeing scenes in his head that amused him. This time he imagined people sitting on the dock putting little hats and dresses and nice little clothes on shiny salmon, halibut, and ling cod. Then a constable coming along and giving them a warning, pointing sternly at the sign. He knew the sign was to keep slimy fish guts off the dock, but still he liked the picture of halibut wearing Toronto Blue Jays sweatshirts and baseball caps.

"Moonbeam," Abby called, looking to the south of Stubbs Island. "I think this might be him."

Down the channel as the fog began to lift, a large white yacht made its way toward the dock. The fog rose like a curtain on cue as the sparkling craft got closer. Moonbeam was mesmerized by the play of light over a ridge of trees that wove a mat of deep green rising up to the tops of Mt. Colnett and Lone Cone, the twin mountains that stood out in the panorama of the sound. The weather had been so lousy ever since they got there that he had forgotten how dazzling the sea-mountain-sky geography was in this place. Super, Natural, British Columbia. They sure got that right.

"Some boat," he whistled.

"More like a ship, eh?" Abby said nervously. "Wave, Moonbeam. So he'll know it's us."

"There's no one else on the dock, Mum." Moonbeam went to the first finger of the dock where Abby was waiting.

"I'm surprised. The tourists aren't as bad as I thought."

"What's-his-name said they don't get really thick until summer."

"His name is *Harvey*."

"I still think we should have set up camp last night instead of staying at *Harvey's* place."

"Like I said, I'm not looking a gift horse in the mouth, Moonbeam. It was pouring."

"If people don't like rain they should live in the prairies."

"You want to move to Calgary or something?"

"No. I don't mind rain. Although the coast sure gets a lot more than Heather Mountain."

"That's over."

"I know that. I'm just saying it's wetter here, that's all."

"Wave." Abby smiled as the boat pulled in next to the dock. "Be friendly."

"You wave." Moonbeam shoved his hands in his pockets as the boat glided smoothly in next to the dock, the engine purring as it idled.

"You folks all set?" A big guy with strawberry-blond hair and a neatly trimmed beard moved quickly to the stern and extended a hand to Abby.

What's with these guys, don't they think she can move around on her own?

Jim Goltz introduced himself and invited them to sit wherever they liked.

"I'll sit up with Jim," Abby said, looking up at the wheel on top of the forward cabin. "Bet there's a great view from up there."

"There's plenty of room if you want to join us, son."

Son? That's weird.

"No, thanks, I'll just stay back here."

Abby and Jim went up top, and in a few minutes the boat backed slowly away from the dock, then turned and headed out of the channel.

Located in Father Charles Channel between Vargas to the north and Wickaninnish to the south, Stere Island was only a short boat trip from Tofino when the weather cooperated. But the Pacific Ocean was rarely calm on this coast of North America. There were rocky islets rising up from the ocean swells, dangerous ocean tides, shoals, wild storms, and the entire shore was often shrouded in the thickest fog. It could get as stormy as the Atlantic, although it didn't share its frigid winters. The Japanese current, the Kuroshio, warmed the shoreline, and the coastal waters were teeming with fish, marine mammals, and sea birds.

A seal popped his head out of the water and peeked at them with big, brown eyes, then darted back down into the ocean. Moonbeam smiled, staring at the spot where the seal had surfaced, hoping the little guy would pop up again.

Even though they had been told the resort was a fancy place, Moonbeam still wasn't prepared for the sight of the sixty-room lodge as they cruised into the marina. Facing north, it was an architectural jewel with large expanses of glass and magnificent stone set in the warmest cedar. He had the impression that the whole place had been dropped there by helicopter and it was somehow just not real.

"Wow," Moonbeam whispered as they walked up the broad steps to the front entrance.

"Yeah, wow," Abby said, nervously. "I'm not sure about this place."

"Not exactly a TraveLodge."

"What are those other buildings?" Abby pointed to a building adjacent to the lodge and then another, about thirty meters southwest of the lodge nestled back in the trees. Both were connected to the ground floor of the lodge with covered walkways.

"The close one is the spa and sport facility. It has exercise rooms, a tennis court, an Olympic-size pool, saunas, and massage rooms," Jim Goltz explained.

Hmmm. Massage. Wonder who gives those?

"Does it have a basketball court?" Moonbeam asked eagerly.

"There is a hoop behind the other building, which is where the employees live. Those that want to live on the island."

Abby stopped just inside the main entrance, glancing appreciatively at the painting over the registration desk. "This lobby looks like an art gallery."

"We have a collection of some of the finest British Columbia Native artists," Jim explained, as Abby stopped by a Native mask next to the huge stone fireplace in the center of the lobby.

"I see you have a Robert Davidson," she said, referring to the famous Haida artist. "My son is actually—"

"How many of the employees live here?" Moonbeam interrupted, glaring at his mother.

"It's about half and half. A lot of people come over from the Ahousat Reserve. Quite a few live in town. Right now there's twelve living in our employee apartments."

"The place with the hoop."

"Right. Why don't I give you a complete tour of the lodge, and then we can go to the office and go over the openings we have."

Before he saw Stere Island Lodge, Moonbeam thought the Empress Hotel had the most beautiful stuff he had ever seen. But this place amazed him. From each table you could see the endless breakers of the open Pacific crashing in on the broad, sandy beach with its storm-tossed driftwood. The island's wild north shore was in such sharp contrast to the fancy dining room with its Emily Carr prints and gleaming silver that Moonbeam again had the weird feeling that there was something unreal about the place.

Off the dining room was a lounge with dark wood paneling and an oil painting of Thomas Stere, one of the early settlers of Clayoquot Sound who first made a famous kayak expedition to the island that was later named for him. Next to the lounge was a small coffee shop and an adjoining gift shop that sold magazines, newspapers, and drugstore items. Across the lobby from the reception desk, Jim pointed out the lodge's exclusive clothing store, Richard Beaupied of Montreal.

"What kind of clothes do they have?" Abby walked toward the shop.

"Pretty pricey. I'm not sure how to describe them. Want to look?"

Abby nodded. She got excited the minute they walked in the shop. "It looks like there's a lot of hand-crafted clothing. Maybe I could talk to them about my weaving!"

A silver-haired lady about sixty, dressed in an expensive sweater and slacks, was looking through the clothes. She peered at Abby and Moonbeam over the top of her glasses and then turned her back, seeming to bristle at the intrusion.

Abby glanced at the price tag of a designer jacket on a rack near the door. "I don't know if they'd want mine." She hesitated, losing her nerve.

"Of course they would, Mum." Moonbeam looked around the shop. "They're as pretty as anything in here."

"Anne Depue, the shop manager, must have stepped out." Jim stood in the doorway and looked across the lobby. "But I'm sure she'd be glad to talk to you."

"Thanks." Abby bit her lip and ran her hand through her hair.

The next stop on the tour was the lodge kitchen, a huge efficient room with large stainless steel appliances. "We've stolen our head chef, Claude Gautier, from the Normandy in Vancouver." Jim introduced them just as a girl who looked about Moonbeam's age emerged from a large pantry. She was at least a head shorter than Moonbeam, with shiny dark hair tied at the nape of her neck in a thick braid. She had a slim, athletic build and moved gracefully in spite of the large sack of potatoes she was carrying.

He's going to introduce me. I will have to say something. I will have to get some words to come out of my mouth.

"This is Gloria Burgess, she's our prep person. But she's been filling in everywhere since we're shorthanded."

"Hi, I'm the potato peeler today," she said, smiling at Moonbeam and Abby.

"Hi, Gloria." Abby greeted her warmly. "Looks like you've got your work cut out for you."

"Hi." Moonbeam tried to look at her, not the floor. "I, uh, used to peel potatoes where we used to live," he said, finally.

"Then you have experience."

"Oh yeah." He looked at the floor. "Me and potatoes are old friends." *I can't believe I just said I have potato friends. Now she thinks I play with Mr. Potato Head.*

"Most of our openings are for the kitchen staff. We've got

to hire a dishwasher right away." Jim Goltz led them into the office down the hall from the lodge kitchen.

"I love to wash dishes," Moonbeam announced enthusiastically.

"You do?" Abby raised her eyebrows. "That's news to me."

"What's your situation with school?" Jim asked. "Would you only be able to work weekends like Gloria does?"

"We had a teacher on Heather Mountain, but it was the same as being home schooled. I have all my assignments until the end of the semester, so I could work full time."

"He's done really well being home schooled. It gives us a lot of flexibility," Abby added.

Yeah and I'm getting sick and tired of it, too.

"We could sure use you." Jim Goltz ushered them into his office. "Pardon the mess on my desk," he apologized, motioning for them to sit down. "Just have a seat and I'll get a couple of applications for you."

He opened a file cabinet, pulled out two applications, and fastened each one to a clipboard. "Take as long as you need. I can answer any questions when I get back. I've got to check on some reservations at the front desk."

Moonbeam bent over the application, printing carefully as he filled in the blanks, steadily moving down the page until he came to the last sentence.

The Stere Island Lodge is situated on land leased from the Clayoquot First Nation People. If you have Native heritage or have Native relatives, please describe below.

Moonbeam looked out the wide glass window toward the wing of the lodge that held the kitchen and dining room. If they got jobs here, they could live right on this island in the staff apartments. It'd be the best of both worlds. A nice little apartment with an inside toilet, but they'd be living right out here on the ocean, with herons and eagles and whales and seals. And that girl Gloria. Someone definitely around his age. Not only around his age, but very, very pretty. She looked to him like she might be Native. Maybe not all, but maybe she was half-Native, like he was, and if he worked here he could get to know her. He'd be an idiot not to do everything he could to get this job! Moonbeam read the sentence again, and then before he had a chance to change his mind, he wrote: Father, Daniel Dawson, Haida, Deceased.

"I'm done," he said, signing his name.

Moonbeam put the clipboard on the desk. Then he saw that Abby was staring at hers and that it was still blank. "How come you haven't filled it out?"

"I need to think about this." She pulled the application off the clipboard and stuffed it in the woven bag she used for a purse. "I'll just do it later."

"What's there to think about? This place is perfect!"

"I need to think about it, that's all."

As they left the marina, Moonbeam sat toward the back of the boat and stared at the lodge. They could actually be living there any day now since Jim said they were in a hurry to get the jobs filled. What a great deal! He could just see himself living in that nice employee apartment place and walking through the forest to the lodge, hanging out in the warm kitchen, eating some of that great food, getting to know Gloria.

When they arrived at the Fourth Street dock, the shift had changed at the Pacific Seafood company and about a dozen sturdy young men in wet olive green slickers and gumboots emerged from the building west of the dock. Sure hope I get hired at the lodge so I don't have to look for work there, Moonbeam thought, imagining a day filled with bloody fish guts. Now that he could see himself on the staff at Stere Island Lodge, every other possible job looked lousy by comparison. But he was afraid to count on it too much.

"What'd you think, Mum?" Moonbeam climbed in the truck.

"This better start." Abby put the key in the ignition.

"Not about the truck, about the lodge."

"Good, it started." Abby put the truck in the gear and headed down Fourth Street.

"So what did you think?"

"It was okay."

"*Okay?* Just *okay?* I'd say it was perfect! I can just see us in those really nice apartments with those huge trees all around. No outhouse, but right out in nature. It couldn't be better. Hey, why don't we stop at that bakery, the Common Loaf?"

"It'll spoil our dinner. Harvey's asked us to eat with him." Abby turned left on Campbell Street and headed out of town.

"Again!"

"Look, we wouldn't even know about the jobs at the lodge if it weren't for him," she bristled.

He knew she was right. And he had to admit so far he didn't seem to be a weirdo. But he still didn't have to like the guy moving in on her so fast. "Okay, but after dinner, we're leaving for the campground."

"Okay."

They rode in silence past the Co-op gas station, MacKenzie Beach Resort, and Ocean Village. Beyond Ocean Village, Moonbeam noticed the surf shop and its large beckoning sign, LIVE TO SURF! Now that's something to try! He could just see it. He'd be all decked out in his jet black wet suit, paddling out beyond the silver breakers on a fine board. His new friends from the lodge would be with him, it would be their day off. He'd catch a big one, carefully mount the board, his legs steady and sure, his arms poised gracefully, balancing him as he expertly rode the wave. The new friends would paddle next to him. They would cheer.

All through dinner at Harvey's, Moonbeam imagined surfing with Gloria and being alone with her at the beach. And as soon as they finished eating, he insisted on doing the dishes. "Might as well get in practice for my new job!"

"Let me give you a hand," Harvey offered.

"No, you made the dinner," he insisted. "Can Gretta have any scraps?"

"Sure, just scrape them into her dish."

Gretta followed Moonbeam into the kitchen and waited patiently by her dish.

"Here you go, girl." Moonbeam patted her head; her dark fur was silky and soft. Great dog, he had to admit, as he scraped the scraps from the plates into her bowl.

Moonbeam looked under the sink for the soap and took it out along with a rack to dry the dishes. This isn't so bad, he thought, as he began swooshing the dish cloth over the dishes. *Swoosh.* Especially when he'd have Gloria to talk to. *Swoosh.* That would be so great. Someone his age, and so pretty, too. *Swoosh.* Nothing to it, washing these dishes! Moonbeam looked out Harvey's kitchen window at the ocean, imagining his life at Stere Island Lodge.

Abby came in the kitchen as he was finishing up. "Moonbeam, I'm exhausted. Harvey said we can stay another night. I'm just too tired to set up camp tonight." She waited, as if bracing herself. "Don't hassle me, *please.*"

Moonbeam started to argue, but then thought better of it. She really did look beat, and after all it was only a matter of time, probably just a few days, before they'd be settled in on Stere Island.

Chapter Four

Mum?" Moonbeam looked at his watch. Eight-thirty. She should be up by now. "Hey, where is everybody?" The house was quiet, the bedroom and bathroom doors were open, and there was no sign of either Harvey or his mother. Where was she anyway, and that guy? Okay, so Harvey wasn't a scumbag, but where had he gone with her so early?

It was a beautiful morning. The spring sun was burning off the mist and the ocean sparkled under the bright sky. Colorado sky. That's what she always called it when there weren't any clouds and the sky seem to glow the color she called cobalt blue. What were they up to, anyway? Moonbeam searched the house, the garage, the shed, the yard, the path, and the beach below; all unsuccessfully.

Might as well eat something, he decided, and went back in the house. That's when he noticed the note on the refrigerator.

Dear Moonbeam,

I have gone with Harvey to look at Palmer's Land near Ellis Lake. We should be back by noon. Harvey said to help yourself to whatever you want to eat. Hope you slept well.

Love,
Mum

Moonbeam opened the refrigerator. Harvey kept plenty of food around, you could say that for him. There were a half-dozen eggs, a pitcher of orange juice, a lot of fancy bottled water, a couple of beers, some cold salmon, lettuce, tomatoes, some leftover pizza, pita bread, cheese, and some mystery food in plastic dishes. Moonbeam settled on the cold pizza. Cold pizza for breakfast was one of his favorites. Although this one had weird stuff on it, he discovered. Not regular pizza-type cheese and pepperoni or sausage. But it still tasted pretty good.

He was finishing his third piece when the phone rang. Moonbeam wasn't sure if he wanted to answer it. He was not thrilled with being Harvey Hattenbach's secretary, taking messages for this guy while he and his mother were out stomping through the bushes, or whatever it was they were doing. But on the fourth ring, he picked it up anyway.

"Hello."

"This is Jim Goltz. I'm calling for the Dawsons."

"This is me, Moonbeam. Hi, Jim."

"Hi, son, is your mother there?"

"She and Harvey went somewhere; they're supposed to be back around noon."

"Well, I can tell you anyway. We'd like you to work for us at the lodge. In fact, the sooner you can start, the better."

"Oh, man, that's great! When do you want us?"

"Actually, tomorrow."

"Cool!"

"We need you in the kitchen, where you'll probably do a bit of everything, dishwasher, prep person, some bussing."

"Hey, you name it. I'll do it."

"We could also use your mother in reservations and reception. She mentioned yesterday that she had worked at the Empress. That's about the best reference we could have. But we need to formally process her application."

"Great! What time do you want us to come tomorrow?"

"First thing in the morning, then if you want to live in the employee apartments we can—"

"We do, we do. That's exactly where we want to live."

"Then you can move your stuff in, get settled, and be ready to work on the dinner shift."

"I don't have that much stuff. I could probably be ready to work lunch."

Jim laughed. "Dinner's fine. The first day is more like on-the-job training and Saturday we'll go over your questions, then take you in town to get the clothes we require for work in the dining room. Unless you already have black slacks and a white shirt?"

"No, nothing like that."

"We'll get you set up. Just be at the boat at the same place tomorrow at nine o'clock."

"Okay, and uh, Mr. Goltz?"

"Jim."

"Right. Jim. Well, there's just one thing. I'm going to change my name. It's not going to be Moonbeam anymore."

"What's it going to be?"

"I'm not sure yet. Maybe you could just call me Dawson, until I get it figured out?"

"Sure, Dawson. Whatever you say, as long as you can handle the work in the kitchen I don't care if you want to be called Humpty Dumpty." Jim chuckled. "See you in the morning, Dawson."

Moonbeam hung up the phone and pounded his fist on the counter. "Y-E-S!" Then he grabbed another piece of pizza. He chewed the pizza, bounced an imaginary basketball, and took his famous hook shot. He could just see himself shooting hoops at Stere Island Lodge, hanging with all his new friends who worked there. He stopped and looked out the kitchen window at Kathryn Bay. Humpty Dumpty. I'm sure. Not funny, buddy. And I'm not your son. But, he grinned, you're the boss. And I've got the job!

Moonbeam finished his breakfast, threw the empty pizza box in the trash, and decided to hitch out to Long Beach. It would be a good place to think about his new name and there didn't seem to be any point in hanging around Harvey's place. Besides, it would be another few hours before his mum got back and he could tell her the great news.

Hitchhiking was a common form of transportation around Tofino. It was the kind of place where people assumed they had more to fear from nature, from wild storms and getting lost at sea, than they did from their fellow humans. Moonbeam figured it was fine to hitch, although his mother had a real thing about it. Growing up in a city in the States, her fear was deeply ingrained. Evil can happen anywhere, she always cautioned him. Although when he got to be in his teens, she finally gave in. As long as he promised never to hitch alone, to always be with at least one other guy.

Well, my name's not the only thing I'm going to change, Moonbeam thought as he left Harvey's place and walked toward the road. There's no other guy around, so I'm hitchin' solo.

He stuck his arm out and walked briskly along the road south to Long Beach. They had camped there when they were here in ninety-three. It was an exquisite stretch of hard-packed white sand adjacent to a Native village on the Esowista Reserve that had existed there for hundreds of years.

Moonbeam heard a car and began walking backwards, so the driver could see him. He tried to look like a decent, friendly person who would be most grateful for a lift. He knew that usually the locals gave each other rides, since everyone knew everyone else in a small town, or at least had seen each other around. Maybe the driver would think he looked familiar. He wanted to look like he belonged here. The car got closer. It was a late-model Honda, a woman by herself. No use. Moonbeam put his hand down.

In a few minutes he heard another one. Walking backwards, he thought it looked like there were two people. Maybe this would be it. He stuck his hand out and smiled like a friendly guy. There were two of them, a couple in a shiny Dodge van who didn't give him so much as a glance. Moonbeam turned around and kept walking, noticing the California plates. It figures, he thought. Tourists would never stop.

Maybe the third time's the charm, he hoped as he heard another car. Moonbeam turned around for his backwards walk, which he was now perfecting, to see that it was a truck. Not only was it a pickup, but it was slowing down! All right! Slowing down and pulling right over. The driver, a burly guy wearing a baseball cap, motioned for him to get in.

"Hey, thanks." Moonbeam opened the door.

"Where to?" The guy looked in the rearview mirror as Moonbeam hopped in, then pulled out into the road.

"Long Beach."

"That's easy. I'm going to Port."

"Are you from around here?" Moonbeam asked.

"Ukee. Been here most of my life."

Moonbeam had actually never been to Ucluelet. He had seen the billboard, UCLUELET: EXPERIENCE LIFE ON THE EDGE, advertising the attraction of Ucluelet's location on the edge of Pacific Rim Park. But most people in Tofino added the phrase "of a clear-cut" to the slogan. Directly across Ucluelet Harbour stood a hideous monument to clear-cut logging, Mount Ozzard. Its barren earth, scarred with desolate stumps and the debris from the mountain's pillage, suggested the devastation of a war; far from attracting tourists, it repelled many, who flocked to Tofino at a rate of about ten to one.

"I've never been to Ukee," Moonbeam said, using the town's nickname.

"Where you from?"

"I lived near Heather Mountain for a while, but I'm going to be from here. I'm moving to Stere Island tomorrow. Got a job at the lodge."

"I hear it's quite the place."

"Sure is." Moonbeam smiled. "Say, do you know anything about Ellis Lake?"

"Like what?"

"Well, like why somebody would go there?"

"As far as I know there's just a campground on the north end. And that hippie place on the south shore. Got a lot of tree huggers and granolas living in shacks there, that's about all I know." He pulled over to the side of the road. "Here's the road to the beach. It's a little less than a kilometer in."

"Okay, thanks a lot." Moonbeam jumped out and waved as the guy pulled out into the road.

Must be a logger, Moonbeam thought, as he watched the truck pick up speed as it rounded the corner then disappeared out of sight. Tree huggers were what they called the environmentalists, and Moonbeam was glad the guy hadn't asked him his name. His new name was going to be a regular name, that was for sure. Tom Dawson had sounded pretty good when he imagined being in the nice foster home with the beautiful daughter, Andrea. But he wasn't sure that was the one he definitely wanted to settle on for his new life at the lodge.

The wind was stronger as Moonbeam walked across the parking lot and along the trail to the beach. As he got closer to the end of the trail, the roar of the ocean got louder. He breathed deeply, filling his lungs with the salty ocean air, then climbed across the huge driftwood lots that had been tossed against the bank from countless winter storms. Shading his eyes he looked north, wondering if he could see Stere Island from here. He could hardly believe it. They'd only left Heather Mountain three days ago and they already had jobs, and not just dumb jobs. Jobs at this fantastic place! What luck!

Moonbeam picked a stick from the driftwood debris and walked across the wide expanse of beach closer to the water where the waves broke over the hard-packed wet sand. He wrote his last name in the sand in big letters. D . . . A . . . W . . . S . . . O . . . N . . . and then began thinking of possible first names. Something quite ordinary and easy to say. Like maybe Tim or Bill or Bob, he decided. Then he took the stick and pulled it through the wet sand, carefully writing the letters of each name.

TIM   DAWSON
BILL   DAWSON
BOB   DAWSON

After writing each entry, he stood back and studied the names in the sand, trying them on for size.

Boring. They were all boring. Maybe a name from sports or some kind of hero would be better than these names. Moonbeam had been a big hockey fan when they lived in Victoria. Even when they lived on Heather Mountain, he and Meadow MacLaine still tried to keep up with the NHL. Meadow's father had a radio that was pretty good, and they could get the games to come through if they took it to a clearing near the highway about a mile from the commune. It was so great sitting out there at night with Meadow, bundled up, stomping up and down to keep warm, and yelling their heads off for the Canucks. Maybe he should think of some of the really all-time-great hockey names. People like Bobby Orr, Gordy Howe, Phil Esposito, Wayne Gretsky (although he had never forgiven him for leaving Canada), and Mario Lemieux. Mario Dawson? Gordy Dawson? Phil Dawson? Hey, maybe he should let fate decide. He would write the initials of each name in the sand where the waves washed up and the first name to be touched by a wave would be the one. Fantastic! His new name chosen by Neptune, God of the Sea.

Moonbeam trotted to the edge of the water and carved a *G* for Gordy (as in Gordy Howe) and *D* for Dawson. He stood with his back to the sea, bent over the sand, so engrossed in carving the initials that when a large wave rolled in, breaking higher on the sand than any of the others, he got caught. Drenched. Completely soaked up to his shins.

"So much for letting fate decide." He trudged back through the sand, his shoes squishing water with every step. Moonbeam looked down at his water-logged feet, imagining a pair of fantastic new shoes. Cool! With this new job there'd be money to get some incredible shoes. Like the players on the Grizzlies wear. It was so great that Vancouver was one of the first Canadian cities to get a team in the NBA. Maybe he could go to Port on his day off with his new friends and watch their games on TV and buy a Grizzlies T-shirt when he got those shoes.

Climbing back over the driftwood at the edge of the beach, he turned to look back at the ocean once more before setting out on the trail. The wind had picked up and the waves rolled into the shore, the white cascading foam spreading in great arcs far up onto the sand. And surfing, too. He'd buy a fantastic board and a wet suit and he and his new friends would head to the beach on their days off. By then he would have forgiven Wayne for leaving Canada and his new name would be Wayne G. (for Gretsky) Dawson. His new friends would call him Wet and Wild Wayne Dawson. He'd be a surfer king. Yes, he definitely liked the sound of that. Wet and Wild Wayne Dawson, King of the Surf.

Moonbeam jogged along the road, deep in thought imagining surfing with his new friends. Many of these new friends were girls who looked wonderful in their wet suits and in the little bathing suits they wore under the wet suits. Maybe one of these new friends would ask him to help her zip up her wet suit.

"Hey, Wet and Wild Wayne," she'd smile sweetly at him, "give me a hand with my zipper, will you?"

"Yeah, Surfer King," her beautiful friend would add, "me, too. I need a little help with my zipper. I seem to be all thumbs."

Moonbeam saw himself reaching for their zippers, helping them get the tight black suits closed around their beautiful bodies in their little bathing suits, when he heard the sound of a loud crashing.

Oh no, she's right. Never should've hitched alone. Maybe it's that logger guy, come back for me. He found out we were at the protests in ninety-three and he's going to hit me over the head with his hatchet . . . then get out his chain saw! More rustling, then another loud crash. Moonbeam froze and stared into the brush.

A black bear stared back at him. Moonbeam tried to think

but his brain was stuck. *They're more scared of us than we are of them.* He could hear his mother's voice. *The only time to worry is if you have food and if they are very, very hungry.* Oh no! What if I smell like the pizza I ate! Maybe he doesn't like goat cheese and artichoke heart pizza. Maybe this is a very traditional bear, only goes for cheese and sausage, or maybe pepperoni. He looks kind of skinny, though. He's probably a young bear, a teenager bear without a lot of experience. Maybe he doesn't know that he's not supposed to eat people. *They're more scared of us than we are of them.* That's what she had told him alright, when they first moved to Heather Mountain and he saw bears for the first time. But he had been six then and she had held his hand. If I move, will he smell the pizza? Maybe he doesn't like garlic. That pizza had a lot of garlic on it. Maybe he's thinking the same thing. Worried that if he moves, I'll shoot him. That I'll want to eat him. *More people hurt bears than bears hurt people.* There was her voice again. Guess the odds are on my side. Moonbeam cautiously took a step forward. He waited a bit, then took another, and with that, the bear turned and disappeared into the brush.

Moonbeam trotted out to the road. Now that it was gone and he was safely back on the highway, he thought it was a pretty cool bear. He stuck his thumb out and walked backwards, but after a bit decided not to hitch. He'd jog back to Harvey's. Seeing that bear had sure gotten his adrenaline going. Moonbeam jogged a little, then began to run. He felt like flying. He was so happy he felt like he could run forever, just keep going and going and going.

He was even happier after a few kilometers when he came to the road to Harvey's house, turned into it, and saw they were back. He couldn't wait to tell her about their jobs! Moonbeam slowed down and then walked the last half of the road to the house, breathing hard, trying to cool down.

"Mum!" He burst in the back door. Abby and Harvey were sitting at the kitchen table having coffee.

"Moonbeam, where were you?" Abby seemed upset.

"Long Beach. I just went out to—"

"Didn't you get my note?"

"Sure. I got it."

"So why didn't you leave one for me?"

"I thought I'd be back by the time you were."

"It's one-thirty. We've been back for almost two hours!"

"I didn't know how long it would take, exactly."

"And how did you get there, I'd like to know!"

Harvey stood up and took his coffee cup to the sink. "I'm going to take Gretta down to the beach. See you later."

"Thanks." Abby smiled at him. "Sorry about this."

Harvey put his hand on her shoulder and then left with Gretta. Moonbeam watched as the door closed behind them. Good. This is none of your business anyway.

"Listen, Mum. I'm back. There's no big deal. I don't want to argue because I've got some great news for us!" Moonbeam grinned.

"So do I." Abby grinned back at him. "So do I."

"You heard, too?"

"Heard what?" Abby was confused.

"About our jobs! That Goltz guy called and they want us both!" Moonbeam dribbled his imaginary ball around the kitchen and took his famous hook shot. "He's picking us up at nine tomorrow and we can move our stuff in those employee apartments. And I'll start work tomorrow night on the dinner shift! Isn't that great?" Moonbeam dribbled across the kitchen toward the hoop at the other end. This time he tried his famous slam dunk. The jam man. Y-E-S! "And all you have to do is fill out the application and they want you to work at the reservations. Just like at the Empress, Mum!"

"Moonbeam," Abby frowned. "Sit down."

"Why? What's the matter?" Moonbeam threw his imaginary ball over his shoulder and leaned against the wall.

"I didn't know Jim Goltz had called."

"Well now you know and we can get our stuff and—"

"Will you please sit down!" she snapped.

"I can talk standing up!"

"Moonbeam, I'm not going to work at that place. I don't want to live there."

"You're kidding, of course." He couldn't believe what he was hearing.

"No, I'm not."

"I don't get it. It's perfect. The lodge only takes up a small corner of the island. The rest of it is wild and completely un-developed. Just what you love. And they have that store where you can sell your weaving."

"I can't stand the people."

"We don't know the people. Only Jim Goltz. What's the matter with him?"

"Not him. The guests. The kind of people who go there, it's what I grew up with, they all have this attitude and I can't stand it. The people from the states are the worst!"

"My whole life you've told me not to judge people with-out knowing them. To give people a chance! And here you are trashing this whole group of people you don't even know!"

"Moonbeam, will you just listen? I found something today that really is perfect for me. It's at Ellis Lake. I met the most wonderful woman, Artis Palmer. She owns about fifteen acres and there are some experimental solar-heated cabins."

"Another friggin' experiment! You've tried it twice, this kind of commune crap, and it doesn't work!"

"This isn't a commune. The cabins are for rent and people are on their own. If they want to pool their resources it's up to them, but you can be as independent as you want. I met some of the people who were here in ninety-three. Moonbeam, I feel like I really belong on Palmer's Land. When I met Artis it was like meeting a kindred spirit." Abby looked at him, pleadingly. "Can't you give it a chance? Just try it?"

"You never once think about me and what I need! I'm sick of being weird and living in the sticks. I want to be with more people my own age."

"I rented the cabin," Abby said quietly.

Moonbeam slammed his fist against the wall. "Fine! 'Cause you're going to live there without me! Jim Goltz will be at the dock at nine o'clock in the morning and you better believe I'm going to be there!"

Chapter Five

The next morning Harvey got up before dawn to get an early start for Sydney Inlet to work on salmon research for the biosphere project. This left Moonbeam and Abby to eat breakfast alone, which they did in complete silence. They had stayed out of each other's way, totally avoiding each other ever since their argument, and still hadn't spoken yet this morning. They sat across from each other, Abby with *The Westerly News* propped in front of her face, and Moonbeam staring out at the gray drizzle. He still wondered if there was a chance she might change her mind, but it seemed easier to start a conversation with the dog than his mother.

"Hey, Gretta." Moonbeam patted her as she waited patiently by his side, hoping for a bit of his breakfast to come her way. "Why don't you come to Stere Island with me?"

"She lives here," Abby said, folding the newspaper back. "She belongs here. She likes it here."

"Yeah, right. Well, maybe they have a nice dog that hangs around the lodge that I can get to know."

"Maybe they will."

The night before, after calling Jim Goltz to let him know what had been decided, Moonbeam had unloaded the truck, removed all his stuff, and then repacked his mother's belongings. Carefully covering everything of hers with the tarp, he took his stuff to Harvey's back door where it would be safe from the rain. The pile of gear was relatively small; Moonbeam didn't have as much as a lot of boys his age. Just his sleeping bag, a duffel bag stuffed with clothes, a basketball, a soccer ball, a Walkman, and a backpack filled with tapes and his school stuff. The classes they had at the Happy Children of the Good Earth had been taught by Meadow's father, who had a B.C. teacher's certificate, but their assignments were processed by the North Island Regional Correspondence School in Port Alberni. Sometimes they were called correspondence kids.

"Sure you have everything for your school work?" Abby got up from the table and kneeled by the pack and started to unzip it.

"It's all there. Don't worry, I don't have to get the next assignment in for another two weeks."

"Well, be sure and do it."

"I always do. Mum?"

"What?"

"Are you sure you don't want to try it there?"

"No. And I know there's no changing your mind, so there's no point in discussing it." Abby looked at her watch. "We best be going."

"You're taking me to the dock?" He was surprised.

"Of course. How did you expect to get there with all that junk?"

"It all fits on my back."

"Don't be ridiculous. Come on, let's go."

They could see the yacht from the lodge coming down the inlet when they pulled into the parking lot. Moonbeam hopped out and began pulling his stuff off the back of the truck.

"I can carry some." Abby came around and stood next to him.

"I've got it, Mum."

"I'll take this," she said, grabbing the basketball.

The boat was a few meters away when they reached the end of the dock. Abby clutched the basketball to her chest, fiercely protective as if it were a newborn baby. Then she ran a hand through her hair and her lower lip quivered.

"Sure you'll be okay?" Moonbeam asked.

"Of course." Her eyes filled with tears.

"Mum, I'll see you every week, on my days off."

Abby wiped her eyes. "I know that."

"Lots of kids will work there this summer and not live at home."

She didn't say anything, just dabbed her eyes.

"Jim Goltz is the supervisor of everyone, it's not like people just run wild. And you'll be coming out to that shop with your weaving. So I'll see you then, too . . ."

She clutched the basketball closer.

". . . and every week, on my day off."

As the boat pulled up, Abby turned away, not wanting Jim Goltz to see her face. He threw Moonbeam a line, then jumped down on the dock.

"This is all, eh?"

"Yeah, I travel light." Moonbeam smiled and picked up his gear.

"If you change your mind about that job, Abby, just give us a call."

"Okay." Abby pulled another Kleenex out of her pocket and blew her nose. "Sure is damp this morning."

Moonbeam lifted the last of his gear onto the boat while Jim held the line.

"Mum?"

"What?"

"Can I have my basketball?"

She handed him the ball. Moonbeam started to toss it on board, but then set it down and reached out to her. She hugged him tightly, clinging to him. "Be careful, Moonbeam."

"I will. You, too."

She stepped back. "I'll be okay." She looked away, trying to hold herself together. "Mind your manners."

"The Queen might be coming, right?"

"She might."

Moonbeam picked up the ball, got the line from Jim, and climbed aboard. "See you soon, Mum," he shouted as the boat backed away from the dock. He stood on the stern and watched the small figure of his mother walk slowly up the hill to their truck and felt his own tears. *Why did she have to be so miserable? It wasn't like he was going to another planet. He'd see her every week. She went away herself to live at that boarding school when she was his age. Why'd she have to make this so hard?*

He worried about her all the way to the island. Any fears he might have had about what lay ahead for him were lost in his worries about her. He'd been looking out for her for as long as he could remember, and he realized that just because he wasn't going to live with her, the worry couldn't be turned off so easily. Like turning off water in a faucet.

As they got farther from Tofino his worries began to get specific. What if there were some rotten, drug-crazed people on Palmer's Land there among the kindred spirits and they would hit her over the head and steal the truck to buy dope? And that Harvey guy, what if he had women all over the place, women everywhere stashed on these little islands he visited for his research project and his mother was just one of hundreds, just waiting for him to dump on her. What if the truck broke down again and this time a deranged cougar with rabies came and mauled her? Or what if a dead tree fell on her cabin and she was pinned under it and there was no one for miles around to help her?

By the time they reached the island, Moonbeam was almost ready to tell Jim Goltz that he had changed his mind. *There's just been a little mistake here, and we have to turn the boat around so I can save my mother from the drug-crazed people and the deranged cougar with rabies. Sorry about this. Nice knowing you. Good luck with the lodge.*

"Moonbeam, grab the line on the cleat, will you?"

"Sure, and it's Dawson. Not Moonbeam, okay?" Moonbeam jumped to the dock and held the stern as Jim brought the bow in close to the dock.

"Right, Dawson it is." Jim threw him the line from the bow and then began unloading Moonbeam's gear. "We're putting you in apartment three, on the ground floor, closest to the kitchen. The top ones are all taken; I guess folks prefer not to have people over them. But it's still pretty quiet."

"Fine by me." Moonbeam hoisted his gear on his back and followed Jim down the dock.

The morning's drizzle had finally let up, but the mist still clung to the island, blurring the horizon and north tip of Stere as the sea and the sky fused together in a mass of gray. Moonbeam looked back in the direction of Tofino, but the mist had rolled in over the dock, obscuring most of the marina. The island seemed even more cut off from everything; a separate, isolated world floating in the fog.

"We still have those few empty units." Jim pointed toward the south end of the employee building. "But I expect they'll be filled in a few weeks when we've got everybody on board." Jim stopped at the last door and took a key out of his pocket. "Nobody locks up much, but when we're at the height of the season it's probably a good idea." He unlocked the door, then handed the key to Moonbeam. "Guess I mentioned the other day that it's furnished. Even the bedding is supplied, and there's laundry facilities at the end of the building."

"This is nice." Moonbeam set his gear down in the tiny living room.

"It's not luxury, but the bed's good and the units are spanking clean. Like everything here, it's brand new."

"It's luxury to me." Moonbeam glanced at the bathroom.

"There's a small store at the end of the marina where you can get supplies, but all your meals are provided."

"Great. What time do you want me to come to work?"

"The kitchen staff reports at three o'clock for the dinner shift."

"Okay."

"If you want some lunch, you can come over earlier. The staff eats at two. But that's up to you. Like I said, there's the marina store if you want to fix food for yourself." He opened the door, then held out his hand to Moonbeam. "Glad to have you part of our team, Moo—uh, Dawson."

"Thanks, thanks a lot." Moonbeam shook his hand. "Mr. Goltz?"

"Jim."

"Jim, I was wondering how long that other job might stay open. The one you thought my mum could do?"

"We hope to get it filled by the end of the week."

"Oh." Moonbeam looked past him through the trees in the direction of the dock, but the fog was thicker and he couldn't even see the water. "That's in just a few days."

"Right. Holler if you need anything, son."

"Thanks." Moonbeam watched Jim Goltz walk toward the lodge. *Son, well I guess I've been called worse things. At least he's not calling me Moonbeam.*

Moonbeam looked around the tiny apartment, which to him seemed immense. All this for only one person. In the bedroom, he unzipped his duffel bag and dumped out his stuff on the bed and started putting his clothes away. Underpants, socks, T-shirts, shorts, jeans, sweatshirts; everything he owned could fit in the top two drawers, with two left over. Sure was different than stuffing everything in the orange crates they had at Heather Mountain. He hadn't had a real dresser in over five years. And a closet. Amazing. He hung up his parka, put his Walkman, tapes, basketball, and soccer ball on the top shelf and then carefully lined up his hiking boots and gumboots on the floor. "Now I've been happy lately . . . thinking about the good things to come." He began to hum as he checked out the bathroom. Everything was so shiny and new. A sign on the wall next to the shower

read: PLEASE CONSERVE. Over the toilet another one said: SEP-
TIC SYSTEM. TOILET PAPER ONLY. "Oh, peace train . . . take this
country . . ." The kitchen cupboards held a set of blue plastic dishes, and a microwave was built in under the cupboard
next to an electric stove top.

The thing about having stuff, Moonbeam thought as he
went back to the bedroom and flopped on the bed, was that
a person had to make decisions. Like do you want to cook on
the stove top or in the microwave. Or should you put your
jeans in the bottom drawer or in the middle. At Heather
Mountain their clothes went in the crate and they cooked on
the wood stove. "Someday it's going to come . . . 'cause out
of the edge of darkness . . . there rides a peace train." He
jumped up and went over to the closet, grabbing his Walkman
from the top shelf and a stack of tapes. On the bed, he sorted
through his tapes. Gotta get that stupid song out of my head.
Wonder what I should do about lunch? Wonder what she's
having? Moonbeam was putting his Walkman on when he
thought he heard a knock on the door. Maybe she changed
her mind. *Moonbeam, Palmer's Land is filled with deranged
dope fiends and a rabid cougar. I want to work here after all;
it'll be just like the Empress. But don't worry, I'll have the apartment at the other end and you can still have this whole thing for
yourself.*

"Hi." Gloria smiled as Moonbeam opened the door.

"Oh, hi—" Moonbeam stood in the doorway, scratching
his head.

"Catch you at a bad time?"

"No, not really."

"I'm the welcoming committee." She looked past him into
the apartment. "I'm Gloria, remember?"

"Oh, sure, I remember." *I must seem like a real jerk, she
thinks I don't remember meeting her.*

"And I forgot your first name."

"Call me Dawson."

"Dawson?"

"Yeah, just Dawson."

"Okay, well, are you going to invite me in?"

"Oh, sure. Sorry."

Gloria closed the door behind her. "This is identical to mine except backwards." She laughed. "I mean every other unit has the kitchen and bathroom reversed since the plumbing has to line up to be back-to-back."

"Oh yeah."

Gloria sat in the chair next to the window. The sun had burned through the fog, and it streamed in through the window, giving her skin a coppery glow.

Moonbeam went to the couch. "Did you know that the water in drains in the northern hemisphere goes clockwise," he blurted, sitting down across from her.

"Drains?" Her dark hair shone in the sunlight. Moonbeam thought it was the shiniest hair he had ever seen.

"Plumbing. You mentioned plumbing." *Oh man, I don't believe it. Here's this good-looking girl, finally one who's my age, right here in my very own apartment, and what do I say? Stuff about drains.*

"Actually, it's the same way with fish."

"What is?"

"They swim clockwise in the northern hemisphere." Gloria smiled, and her dark eyes sparkled. "They never teach you stuff like that in school, though."

"I guess not."

"Where did you last go to school, Just?"

"Just?"

"Isn't that your name?"

"What name?"

"Just Dawson, I thought it was your nickname. Just for Justin." Gloria looked confused. "Isn't your name Justin Dawson?"

Moonbeam laughed.

"What's so funny? I didn't get your name right?"

"No, I mean yes, that's what I said, 'just Dawson.' "

What a jerk. I'm not making any sense at all. Moonbeam looked down at the floor trying to figure out what to say, then he looked up at Gloria. Her eyes were steady and warm, and they seemed to smile.

"See my mum calls me this stupid nickname, and, well, I hate my real name, too. Dawson is my last name and it's okay, but I didn't want anyone here to use my first name until I picked a new one."

"What's your real name?" Gloria asked.

"I never tell anyone."

"Oh. So what name do you want to be called here?"

"I'm not sure yet. I was thinking maybe Wayne, for Wayne Gretsky, or Gordy, for Gordy Howe."

"You play hockey?"

"Not really. A little floor hockey when we lived in Victoria, that's all. But that was a long time ago."

"Jim told me you were part Haida, right?"

"I guess so. Why?"

"You don't know for sure?"

"Mum says my dad was Haida. I didn't know him."

"Well, I was just thinking it might be nice to tie that in somehow." Gloria gathered her hair and twisted it in a thick braid. She seemed to be giving serious consideration to his new name.

"You're Native, right? Or part?" They were having such a personal conversation, it seemed like he might as well ask her.

"No. My dad's white and my mum's Japanese, but from here. Japanese-Canadian. But most people think I'm Native or part Native, especially at the lodge since they want to hire first nation people. Also because of my last name. There's a well-known Native artist in Tofino whose last name is the same as mine, Burgess."

"The guy with that cool gallery?"

"That's Roy Henry Vickers. The Eagle Aerie Gallery. Ralph Burgess is Tsimshian; he carves jewelry. His stuff is at the other gallery that's native-owned, the House of Himwitsa."

"I've gone in there; it's nice."

Gloria stood up and looked at her watch. "It's almost two. I'm going to go eat with the staff, want to come?"

Moonbeam jumped at the invitation. Now he wouldn't have to decide whether or not to eat with the staff or go down to the marina store and get something. Although he knew he probably would have gone to the marina store. Walking into a group of people who all know each other can be pretty weird. But now he could go with Gloria.

Once again, he couldn't believe his good luck. She had actually come over to meet him, and now here he was going with her to the main building. He was walking next to this very pretty girl, someone his own age. And even more than that, someone that was easy to talk to. Amazing.

Rain dripped from the canopy of cedar boughs that sheltered the path, and the wet branches glittered as the sun filtered through them. Moonbeam could hear voices echoing from the marina down below, but other than that, and the sound of small birds and chipmunks rustling in the brush, it was quiet where they walked.

Halfway to the lodge, Gloria suddenly stopped. "Shh . . . look!" She put her hand on his arm and pointed to the highest branch of a tree slightly to the west of them. "See?"

There was no mistaking the pure white head, the massive brown breast of the eagle. "It's an omen, I think," Moonbeam whispered.

"There are a lot of eagles around, but I've never seen one this close to the lodge. Maybe he's welcoming you."

Moonbeam stared up at the magnificent bird. The sun was behind the eagle, its rays spiking through the branches like shards of golden glass as if the bird were the center of a sunburst.

"My dad was from the Eagle clan," Moonbeam whispered.

"I thought you didn't know much about him?"

"I don't really, but my mum told me once about the Eagle clan and I just remembered it, I guess."

"I've got an idea," Gloria whispered. "Have you been in the gift shop?"

"Jim pointed it out when I was here the other day, but we didn't go in."

"Come on. I want to show you something."

In the gift shop, Moonbeam followed Gloria to a rack of postcards next to the far wall. They looked like the usual tourist stuff to him. Orca whales, sandy beaches, a colony of sea lions on some rocks, snow-capped mountains framing the deep green of the old growth forest, a bear and her cubs, someone holding a 30-pound Chinook salmon, and WELCOME TO CANADA with a big red maple leaf. Moonbeam spun the rack. "You want me to look at one of these?"

"No, here." Gloria pointed to a shelf of books behind the postcard rack and pulled out a large book with a beautiful cover, the kind people put on a coffee table in their living room. "This is what I wanted you to see."

"Indians of the Northwest Coast." Moonbeam stood next to her and read the title. "Cool mask." He pointed to the cover photo of a vivid mask and its bold red, gold, black, and white colors. "What about it?"

"Just wait." Gloria looked in the index, then flipped through the pages to one with a photograph of a sculpture. "This." She pointed to the photo.

"I've seen that before somewhere."

"It's in the museum in Vancouver. At U.B.C."

"Mum took me there when we lived in Victoria."

Moonbeam stared at the photograph. A large raven stood on top of a giant shell that opened to show a tiny human form emerging from the shell. Next to the photograph it told about the myth on which the sculpture was based:

Raven Yel was walking along the beach one day. He was bored, and in his irritation he called to heaven, which to his surprise, answered him, although it was only a muffled croak. Curious, he looked around and saw a giant shell at his feet. It opened a crack and he saw that it was full of tiny beings who were peering out fearfully. Yel was happy for the diversion and began to coax with the gentle tongue of the schemer, enticing and urging the inhabitants of the shell to come out and play with him. It was not long before first one being and then the others, shyly and fearfully, ventured out of the shell. They were strange creatures: two-legged like Raven Yel, but without his shining feathers. Covered only with pale skin, they were naked except for the long black hair on their round, beakless heads. Instead of wings they had sticklike appendages. But Yel was satisfied and very happy with his new playmates—the first people.

"I know about this. We studied a lot of the Native myths and legends when I lived on Heather Mountain." Moonbeam handed the book back to Gloria. "I don't exactly get what it has to do with me."

"Here's the caption." She pointed to a small paragraph, then read it to him. "The Haida myth retold on the opposite page finds its most beautiful visual expression in this sculpture created by artist Bill Reid."

"Okay, so it's Haida, but . . ."

"Bill Reid is half-white and half-Haida."

"Like me."

"So I thought maybe that would be a good name."

"Bill Dawson?"

"Why not?"

"It's one I've been considering. That and Tom." Moonbeam looked at the caption again. "Hey! I've got it. Reid. Spelled the same as his."

"Hmmm, I like it." Gloria smiled approvingly. "It's better than Bill Dawson."

"It's better than Just Dawson," he laughed. Then he looked

at the book again, studying the sculpture intently, staring at the smooth, expertly carved lines.

"Reid Dawson, that's it," he announced, decisively snapping the book shut. "That's my new name!"

Chapter Six

The first time Moonbeam introduced himself as Reid, he couldn't believe how normal it seemed. It really surprised him since he'd been imagining there might be this big reaction. Someone would say, "Ha! You're a fake and we all know it. *Reid* Dawson? No way! We all know your real name is weird, and it's *Moonbeam*." But instead Claude, the head chef, said, "Nice to meet you, Reid." The hostess, Joan Dublanko, shook his hand. "Hi, Reid. How are you?" And Dorothy Baert, one of the servers, welcomed him warmly, "Hello Reid." Even Jim Goltz was very casual about it when he stopped in his office to make it official.

"Hi, Dawson, how's it going?"

"Fine. Oh, by the way. I'm going to be called Reid now."

"Your first name?"

"Yeah, Reid Dawson. I'd like to change it on my application if I could."

"No problem." Jim went to the file, pulled out the application, and handed it to him. Moonbeam crossed out Moonbeam and wrote Reid. That was all there was to it.

After he left Jim's office, he headed straight to his apartment, right to the bathroom, and right to the mirror. "Hi, I'm Reid," he said to the mirror, staring at his own face. Was it just his imagination, or did he actually look different? *Pretty strange, eh?* he thought, studying his face. *My name changes and then my face?* But he was sure of it. Something was different. He looked stronger somehow and not so much of a kid. Not like a kid with a weird name.

Reid wondered about his friends from Heather Mountain. Meadow MacLaine, Rainbow Callanti, and that pest, Starlight Lewis. Where had they ended up? Who would have thought that he would be here at this fancy resort, a new place, with a new name. *Reid Dawson.* After introducing himself, "Hi, I'm Reid Dawson," about sixty-three times to the mirror, he left the bathroom to practice writing it.

Reid got his paper and school stuff from the bedroom closet and took them to the kitchen table. R-e-i-d D-a-w-s-o-n, he wrote carefully. Then he wrote it again, copying his new name on every line, until he had filled the page. Even his handwriting seemed a little different, as if it were stronger, too, and less like a kid's.

The next step is to make it official with the correspondence school, he decided, taking a clean sheet from his notebook. He thought about asking Jim if he could use the computer in the office so it could be typed all nice, but that seemed like too much of a hassle. He just went ahead and wrote it.

> *Reid Dawson*
> *Stere Island Lodge*
> *P. O. Box 933*
> *Tofino, BC VOR 2Z0*

District Administrator
North Island Regional Correspondence School
Port Alberni, BC

Dear Administrator:

Please change my name on all your records. It used to be Moonbeam Dawson. I am in the Grade 10 correspondence program. My name is now Reid Dawson. Thank you very much.

> *Sincerely,*
> *Reid Dawson*

He read over the letter and decided to send it from Tofino when he went to get the slacks and shirt at the Co-op. Maybe he'd stop in and see his mother, too, since he didn't have to be back at the lodge until the dinner shift. Probably her loom and everything she owned was still on the truck just waiting for him to unload it, and it would be good to help her right away instead of waiting for his first day off. As he imagined her stuck out there alone in the wilderness, the scene became so vivid in his mind, Reid got a knot in his stomach. He tried to think of something else, like surfing with his new friends, but it didn't help.

He bent over and held his hand on his stomach, hoping that might fix it. When he had stomachache when he was a little kid, she gave him peppermint tea and told him this story she made up. "Lois the Rabbit and the Magic Ingredients." Lois the Rabbit was afraid of this wolf named—Reid thought for a moment. What was the name of that wolf anyway? He couldn't remember, but the wolf was afraid of everything—even rabbits—and this wolf only ate veggies, never meat. Lois the Rabbit lived nearby and was afraid of the wolf. Then the two of them bumped into each other near a pretty plant with golden leaves. The leaves had magic ingredients. And then Lois the Rabbit and this wolf, whatever-his-name-was, ate the leaves. The magic ingredients were acceptance, courage, and love, and then the rabbit and the wolf got to be friends and went through life eating veggies. Reid rubbed his stomach. He'd have to remember to ask her that wolf's name.

After a while his stomach began to feel better, so he got his basketball and went to the court behind the building to shoot some hoops. He had about twenty minutes before he had to be at work, and he wanted to run around a bit.

And now! Ladies and gentlemen, the starting lineup for the Vancouver Grizzlies!

Reid trotted out to the center of the court and waved at the trees. *At forward, Reid Dawson! A roar goes up from the crowd. The Grizzlies begin warming up.*

Reid ran toward the basket and shot. *Reid Dawson dazzles the crowd. Every shot goes in. His famous hook, the jam, the world-renowned Dawson Dunk!*

Then he went back to the center of the court and proudly held the ball at his side, facing the trees, his back to the lodge. *And now, ladies and gentlemen, please stand for the national anthem. "Oh, Canada, our home and native land . . . true patriots love, in all our sons command . . ."*

"Throw it here, eh?" Gloria smiled.

Reid jumped, surprised by the sound of her voice. "I didn't see you." He grinned, feeling a little foolish, then tossed her the ball.

She dribbled a few times, then let go of her shot. "You were pretty involved."

"Hey, you're good." He grinned again, watching it sail through the hoop.

"Don't act so surprised."

He got the ball and passed to her, secretly wondering if she'd just gotten lucky. He hadn't thought of her as a jock. But her second shot went in just as easily.

"You play on a team or something?"

"I did, before I got this job. I only work here on the weekends, but most of the games are on Friday and Saturday so I had to quit the team."

"What team?"

"Girls Varsity at U.S.S." Gloria passed to him.

"What's that?" Reid's jump shot missed by a mile. "I'm pretty rusty." He laughed as he chased the ball out of the bushes behind the hoop and threw it to her.

"Ucluelet Secondary School. I'm in grade ten."

"Is it big?"

"There's grades eight through twelve. About two hundred fifty in the school. We've got about fifty in my class."

"I've been home schooled for the past five years, although we had something like a school on Heather Mountain."

"I wish I could do that. I don't feel like I'm much a part

of things at school since I board out here on the weekends."

"That's funny." Moonbeam dribbled the ball in place and looked at her.

"What is?"

"That people always want something different. I've been thinking about regular school. Does everyone come from Ukee?" Moonbeam dribbled the ball over to the edge of the court and sat down next to her.

"Ukee and from Opitsat on Meares Island, the Native reserve at Long Beach, and some from the Port Albion area. It's called Ucluelet East across the harbour from Ukee. And Tofino, too."

"Kids who live in Tofino take a bus to U.S.S.?"

"That's right." Gloria looked at her watch. "Guess we'd better be getting to work."

"Yeah, that's all I'd need, be late on the first day." He stood up and looked over toward the main building.

"Hey, Reid, pull me up." Gloria smiled up at him, holding out both her hands. He wasn't sure what surprised him more, answering so easily when she called him Reid or holding her hands.

"Have you heard what they're saying about us?" Gloria's dark eyes sparkled as he pulled her up.

"About us?" Reid picked up a stick as they walked along the path, trying to seem casual.

"Joan and Dorothy. They said we look so much alike we could be brother and sister, or at least cousins."

"They think I look like a girl, eh?"

"No, that's not what they meant. They said you were a good-looking guy."

Reid felt embarrassed. He stopped and broke the stick over his knee as Gloria walked ahead of him. After a minute he trotted up to her, and announced, "Well, you're not so bad."

"What a great compliment." Gloria burst out laughing. "And I suppose it means I look like a guy!"

"No way. You're really, uh," he mumbled, "you're really pretty." They had arrived at the employee entrance of the kitchen.

"I'm certainly glad I forced that out of you," she said in a mock, snippy voice as she opened the door.

All Reid could see was the back of her head as he followed behind her. Maybe he'd really insulted her. *The first girl he'd met his own age since Victoria, and he'd already said the wrong thing!*

He wrote his name on the sign-in sheet underneath hers. When he looked up, she was standing next to him.

"I'm, uh, sorry," he mumbled.

"For what?" She seemed surprised.

"About what I said."

"Huh?"

"That you weren't so bad."

"Oh, please," she laughed. "I was kidding."

Oh, man. How're you supposed to know what's going on?

"Here," she smiled as she handed him a menu. "We have a tradition here that Claude had when he was at the Normandy. When it's your first day at work, you get to pick anything on the menu for your own dinner."

Gloria stood close to him, looking at the menu with him. She put her hand on his arm. "This is great. The cappellini with sautéed prawns, tomato, garlic, and tarragon. I had it my first day."

He felt the warmth of her hand on his arm. *He'd gotten all bent out of shape for nothing!* "What's cappellini?"

"It's pasta."

There were a bunch of weird names of stuff he had never heard of, caponata, bruschetta, portabello, confit, he couldn't believe the stuff they had on that menu.

"You pick for me." He handed the menu to Gloria.

"No, it's your dinner."

"You helped me pick my name, you can pick my food."

"Okay, Reid. But I get a bite."

"Of course, I always share with my sister." He laughed, trying to make a joke. But as soon as he said it, he started to worry. *Why had she told him somebody said they looked like brother and sister? Was that a clue that she only wanted to be friends? Like a sister or something?*

"Start with the mushroom and wild rice soup, then have the baby spinach salad with roquefort, walnuts, and the honey-sherry vinaigrette, and have the herb-roasted chicken and the garlic mashed potatoes for your entree."

"Do we get dessert?"

"Have the chocolate hazelnut torte, but I get at least three bites."

"Two, max."

"Okay, two."

In the beginning the work didn't seem that hard. Washing, peeling, and slicing the vegetables, trying to anticipate Claude and how he wanted everything done; it all seemed pretty manageable. But compared to Gloria, he was slow with the knife and after about a half-hour Claude switched him to washing and tearing the lettuce, wild greens, and spinach. He said to make small, bite-size pieces, and Claude periodically checked it over to make sure Reid wasn't tearing them too big and that they were completely clean.

Reid worked steadily next to Gloria over a huge, long stainless steel sink. Claude told them he didn't mind if they talked as long as the work was done properly. It wasn't that boring. He got to be close to her and while he was cleaning the spinach, she told him a lot about her background.

"My great-grandfather's name was Saburo Yamada. His family came to Canada in the late eighteen hundreds, although I'm not sure of the exact year, but they were among the first Japanese in North America and he was born in Vancouver around nineteen hundred. He even fought in the Canadian Army in World War I and was sent to France."

"Really?" He liked listening to her, it was interesting. Also, it meant he didn't have to talk, so there was less chance he'd mess up.

"After the war, he settled in Clayoquot Sound and worked as a fisherman. He and his wife had three kids, and my grandmother was the oldest." Gloria pointed to the counter. "Hand me that knife, will you?"

"This one?"

"Yes, thanks." She began slicing tomatoes into even, beautiful slices. Reid watched her hand making smooth, rhythmic strokes with the knife. She made it seem effortless.

"My grandmother tells a story about her father during World War II when the government took the boats that belonged to all the fishermen of Japanese descent. He had fought with the Seaforth Highlanders and on the day they took all the boats, he put on his regiment's uniform and went down to the dock and was standing there in the Scottish tam and jacket with its brass buttons buttoned up when they came." She stopped slicing and looked over at Reid. "After that their family was sent to the interior with all the other Japanese-Canadian families from the coast. She doesn't talk much about that part. She just says *shikataganai.*"

"What's that?"

"*Shikataganai* means something like 'what can you do?' Like there's nothing that can be done so you just accept it. It's one of the few Japanese words I know."

"Were they put in one of those camps?"

"Yes, but no one in my family says much about it. They ended up in Toronto after the war, and then in 1952 BC Packers recruited the Japanese-Canadian fishermen to come back to the coast. That's when the family settled in Ukee." Gloria went to the large walk-in refrigerator and filled the colander with more tomatoes. "What's really sort of odd is that my dad worked for Tohei, the Japanese packing company, until they closed. Now he's at the Clayoquot Fish Company, but he had been at that Japanese company a long time."

"And your dad's Canadian."

"Mum's Canadian, too," she snapped. "Color and citizenship aren't the same. That's the whole point."

"I know," he said, feeling stupid. "I just meant your dad's white."

She nodded. "He's from Port. He and my mum met at university."

The first seating in the dining room was at 5:00, and within twenty minutes the orderly efficiency of the prep work gave way to what seemed to Reid near chaos. The air became tropically thick with vaporized food particles sprayed off dirty plates with 140-degree water, the floor tiles became slippery, and everyone was sweating. Their damp shirts stuck to their backs. Orders spewed out of the high-speed printer and were slapped on the counter as line cooks grabbed the tickets and shouted to the preppers to pull the food from the walk-in. "Reid! One caprese!" "Gloria! Two escarole!" "Reid! Zuppli! Five for the five top!" "Gloria! Four spinach!" He heard his name what seemed like a thousand times from the line cooks while he staggered under huge trays of lemon wedges, plucked pomegranate seeds, and ground coriander, and he was still trying to learn what all the stuff was.

It didn't die down until 10:00. Reid chopped the last of the shallots and skewered the shrimp. Next to him Gloria sprinkled powdered sugar on plates that would hold Claude's signature dessert, a dacquois, layers of baked meringue filled with buttercream and topped with shaved chocolate.

"Is it always like this?" Reid arranged the skewers on a large stainless broiler pan.

"It has been since I started, but I'm only here on weekends. I'm not sure about the middle of the week."

"This is a lot harder than I thought." He carried the pan to the line cook and came back over to her.

"First day's always the worst." She sprinkled the shaved chocolate over the dacquois.

"Who knows what I would have brought out if you hadn't pointed to the stuff they wanted in the fridge. I never heard of half of this stuff." Reid leaned back against the counter. "Thanks," he said, genuinely grateful.

"I look out for my friends," she smiled. "But remember, I'll collect when you get your dessert."

Friends. There it is again. But this time it's loud and clear. She only wants to be friends.

"When do we eat?" he asked, trying to hide his disappointment.

"I think Claude has your entree ready now. We eat at the corner table by the sideboard after the last guests leave."

By 10:15 the dining room was empty and Reid got his food from Claude and sat next to Gloria at the corner table. Friends was a lot better than nothing, he decided as he pulled his chair next to her. A lot better.

"This is incredible." He tried to eat slowly so he could remember each bite forever, because he had never tasted anything like this food.

"My turn." Gloria picked up her fork and started to go for his plate.

Reid put his hand on hers and laughed. "Just a minute! Are there any rules on how big the bites are?"

"Yes. As big as I want." She took her hand away from his and cut into his dessert. "Mmmm . . . yum." Gloria half closed her eyes, relishing the scrumptious chocolate torte.

"I feel sort of bad eating this great stuff." Reid looked at the cake.

"Why? You worked your butt off in there, you sure earned it."

"I was just thinking about all the boring stuff my mother eats." He finished the dessert and then stood up and began clearing their plates. "Guess I'll turn in. Jim has to catch a ferry at Nanaimo so he's going to take me to the Co-op first thing in the morning."

Reid was so tired from his first day at work, he fell asleep the minute his head hit the pillow, but instead of sleeping soundly until his alarm went off at 6:30, he woke up at 5:30. He thought he'd heard someone crying. He sat up in bed, not knowing where he was for a minute. Groping for the light, he turned it on and looked around the room. His apartment. Stere Island Lodge. No sound of anyone. He'd been dreaming.

He had been sitting at a huge table covered with food, plates and plates of incredible food, like a feast in a palace. He was so excited to eat it, he hardly knew where to begin. He decided to start with dessert, a beautiful chocolate cake. But just as he took a bite, he noticed a grungy person locked outside, peering in the window. He tried to give the person some food, but the window was stuck.

Reid tried to go back to sleep, but after a few minutes of tossing and turning decided it was hopeless. He showered and got dressed and headed over to the kitchen for some breakfast. Except for the lobby and the lights in the kitchen, the lodge was still dark. Jim was having breakfast when he got there.

"Your mother called last night, Reid."

"She did?" He got some cereal and sat next to Jim.

"Wanted to make sure you'd know how to get to her new place today. In case you decided to stop in after the Co-op."

"It's on the edge of town on Ellis Lake, right?"

"Right. She said it's at the end of the north fork of the road that goes into Palmer's Land from the highway. You can walk there pretty easily."

Reid couldn't finish his cereal. He had that stupid knot in his stomach again. He wanted to ask Jim how she'd sounded, but he didn't dare. The truth was that he really didn't want to know. Judging by how she was yesterday, she probably sounded bad.

When they got to town, Jim went in the Co-op with Reid and signed for the slacks and shirt on the lodge account, then he left for Nanaimo while Reid was trying the clothes. By the time he'd finished at the Co-op it had started to rain. It was coming down hard and the idea of his mother alone in the cabin in the rain made him feel terrible. The rain was relentless, and by the time he walked out to Palmer's Land there were strong gusts of wind hammering the rain down in vast sheets. It was more like a winter storm down from Alaska. There were few cars on the road between Tofino and Ellis Lake, not even a dog in sight in the rough weather.

Reid pulled the hood of his parka lower over his head as he turned into Palmer's Land. The narrow dirt road was muddy with thick, deep tire tracks and he thought someone could easily get their car or truck stuck here. He was picturing her in their truck, the tires almost submerged in mud and no one around for miles to hear her, when he spotted some lights through the trees. It looked like there was a cabin back in there.

As Reid rounded a bend in the road, he saw their old pickup parked next to a small cedar structure, an interesting modern design with a roof of large solar panels. Reid noticed the truck's tires were muddy and the faded bumper sticker, ARMS ARE FOR HUGGING, was so mud-splattered you could hardly read it. But the truck itself didn't look any worse for wear, and to his surprise it was completely unloaded. Through the window he could see a cozy fire in the fireplace. As he stepped up on the porch, about to knock, the door swung open.

"Moonbeam!" Abby squealed and threw her arms around him.

"Hi, Mum."

"Well, come on in. Let's have a look at you!"

"I don't think I've changed. I just saw you yesterday."

"Well, it seems a lot longer." Abby closed the door behind him. "Have a seat. Here's the rocker, right by the fire. Are you hungry? Can I get you anything, Moonbeam?"

I have a new name now and it's Reid.

"Maybe later." He sat in the rocker and looked around the room. It looked like she'd been living in the cabin forever the way everything had been put away. Even the loom was in the corner. "How'd you get that up?"

"Harvey helped me. By midmorning yesterday we had the entire truck unloaded. He was great."

"Oh."

"Then he chopped a cord of wood for me and stacked the whole thing by the side of the cabin. He was really wonderful." Abby went to the small kitchen at the end of the cabin and took the hot water off the hot plate. "Want some tea? Harvey's got this wonderful spice blend he let me have."

"Maybe later." Reid picked up a pamphlet on the table next to the rocker and looked at the title. "Bear Alert!" he read aloud. "What's this?"

"Artis Palmer's part of it and I'm going to get involved, too."

"Involved in what?" *Now* what is she up to? he wondered as he looked at the pamphlet.

"Bear Alert wants to stop the slaughter of black bears in Clayoquot Sound. Also the poaching that's part of the illegal trafficking in bear body parts."

"Who wants bear body parts?" Reid frowned, skeptical.

"It tells all about it," Abby said from the kitchen.

Reid sighed and read the pamphlet.

BEAR ALERT!

Currently in British Columbia, guide outfitters conduct hunts which can hardly be called hunting by any sporting definition. So-called hunters from the United States and Europe pay outfitters three thousand dollars for a guaranteed kill. This "sport" takes place in the spring, the time when unsuspecting bears head for the beaches to feed on crabs and other seafood.

Easy targets, the bears, animals known to have poor eyesight, are groggy from hibernation to the extent that they are rendered practically blind. The "hunters" cruise the shore in boats and shoot the nearly blind bears while they're feeding on the beach. This practice is currently legal in British Columbia.

Educating the public regarding the illegal practice of trafficking in bear body parts is also the aim of **Bear Alert!** Bear body parts, particularly bear gall, the bear's gall bladder, have proven medicinal value and can be worth up to eighteen times the price of gold in Asia and Asian communities in North America. However, there are synthetic and herbal alternatives every bit as effective. Using these alternatives and stopping the demand for bear body parts will save this unnecessary slaughter of bears.

Bear Alert! is working in the Asian communities to present the herbal and synthetic alternatives to bear gall. Asian bears are practically extinct, and unless the slaughter is stopped here, bears will become dangerously close to extinct in North America.

"So what are you going to do about it? Hand out these pamphlets to warn the bears?" Reid put the pamphlet back on the table.

"It's *not* funny, Moonbeam." Abby carried her tea in from the kitchen.

"Just a little joke."

"Well it's serious."

"Okay, okay," Reid muttered.

"And for your information Bear Alert does try to warn the bears by intercepting the trophy hunters and poachers. Making a lot of noise to warn the bears that the so-called hunters are coming."

"So you and these people run around in the bushes blowing whistles and stuff."

"I'm not going to talk about this if you think it's so bloody funny." Abby went back in the kitchen. "Listen, how 'bout some lunch? I've opened a jar of that blueberry jam we put up last spring."

Reid grinned at the mention of blueberry jam. He hadn't come out here just to argue with her, and at least blueberry jam was something they could agree on. He followed her into the kitchen. "There isn't any jam at the lodge as good as yours."

Abby reached up and tousled his hair. "Pretty soon I won't be able to reach the top of your head."

"Just don't do that in public," he warned, with a slight smile.

"I'm coming out to the lodge next week. I'm getting some samples together to take to Anne Depue at the shop. Harvey's going to take me over."

"I can show you my apartment."

"Great. Say, how's the food?"

"It's fabulous."

"A lot of meat, I suppose." Abby spread jam on the bread. "Is there anything I can say to convince you not to eat it?"

"No."

"Nothing, Moonbeam?"

"I've heard your meat speech my whole life." *And it's Reid now, too.*

Abby looked upset as she handed him the sandwich.

"Thanks." He took a bite of his sandwich.

"Sure."

"Hey, what's the name of that wolf?"

"What wolf?"

"The wolf from that story you used to tell me. The one about 'Lois the Rabbit and the Magic Ingredients,' where the rabbit and the wolf ate the leaves with the magic ingredients."

"Acceptance, courage, and love, and then they were friends and ate veggies."

"Yeah, that wolf."

"Clarence."

"Oh, right. I remember. Lois the Rabbit and Clarence the Wolf." Reid stuck his knife in the jam and spread some on another piece of bread. "Wolves are supposed to be endangered, too. Are you trying to protect them?"

"Not in an organized way like with the bears."

"Well, just be careful," he warned, in his parental voice. "When the logging roads were blockaded in ninety-three, the whole world was watching. But trying to scare off redneck trophy hunters out there alone could be dangerous."

"We don't go out alone."

"Listen, Mum," Reid set his knife down. "Just be careful."

Chapter Seven

Reid was getting dressed, getting ready to go to the kitchen to set up for breakfast, when he heard a knock on the door.

"Just a second," he yelled, pulling his T-shirt over his head.

Reid ran to the door. It was Jim Goltz. "I need you to fill in for one of our bellhops. Brad Wellman's out with the flu."

"So I shouldn't report to the kitchen?"

"Not until tonight. Claude will have you bus tables. At three-thirty we need you down on the dock to meet a float plane. Just greet the guests, take their bags to registration, then show them to their room."

"That's all?"

"In the room, open the cabinet and show them the TV and VCR and tell them we have complimentary videos at the front desk. There's a small refrigerator that's stocked with drinks and snacks. You'll have the key to it, and you just open it to show them and then give them the key. It's pretty straightforward."

"Okay. I'll go down at three-thirty."

"Right." Jim turned to leave. "Say, how'd it go with your mum? You didn't say much on the way back yesterday. She like Palmer's Land okay?"

"It was fine." Reid tried to sound casual. "She seems to be all set there."

Actually, his visit had left him sort of mixed up. It was a relief to see that she was doing fine, that he could just live his life and not have to worry about her so much. But she hadn't asked him to do anything to help her. Not a single thing. That Harvey guy seemed to have just taken over.

Down at the dock Reid heard the engine of the float plane. He looked up and saw the sun gleaming against the wings as it glided toward the marina. The black-and-white Wickaninnish Air logo, an orca whale, shone against the silver fuselage as the big pontoons touched down, sending arcs of salt spray cascading across the water. From the cockpit, Joe Martin waved to Reid as he brought the plane within inches of the dock. A perfect landing.

There were just two passengers. A guy with silver hair who looked like he was in his forties. And right behind him, just about the most beautiful girl Reid had ever seen. She didn't look anything like the girls he and Meadow saw in Port Alberni, or even like Gloria, who was very pretty. This girl was dazzling. Like a movie star or something. He stared at her, holding the door of the plane as she climbed down to the dock. He felt immobilized, completely forgetting for a minute why he'd been sent there in the first place. Joe motioned to their luggage: two medium bags and a fishing rod case. Reid put a bag in each hand, then got the case up under his shoulder, and prompted by Joe, blurted, "Welcome to Stere Island Lodge!"

"Oops!" As he turned away from the plane, pivoting with the luggage, the fishing rod case whacked the silver-haired guy in the back. "Oh, no! Sorry!"

"Watch it." The guy put his hand on the case. "Maybe I'd better carry that."

"No, sir, I'm really sorry. I've got it. Just lost my balance. Sorry, sir. Just follow me, sir."

Great first impression. Here's this beautiful girl and the first thing I do is ram her old man with his fishing rod. Reid led the way up the stairs from the dock, convinced they were smirking at him behind his back with every step.

When Reid got to the main entrance he set their luggage down, then opened the door. "The registration desk is to your right."

"Thanks." The girl smiled as he held the door. Then she followed her father inside. Her face was only a few feet from his as she passed through the doorway. He felt his cheeks get hot. Her smile was radiant, the kind of smile you'd see in a toothpaste commercial, and she had these incredible eyes, like a cat's. They were light brown or maybe light green with gold flecks sparkling in them and along with her long, thick, honey-blond hair, she looked like she probably really *was* a model.

Reid got their bags and the fishing case and carried them to the registration desk where Jim Goltz was checking them in.

"Reid." Jim motioned to him. "This is Robert Lamont and his daughter, Michelle. They'll be with us for the week. This is Reid Dawson, he's a bit of a jack-of-all-trades around here."

"Yes, he welcomed us at the dock." Mr. Lamont winked at his daughter.

Jim handed their keys to Reid. "Show the Lamonts to Room 426."

"Just follow me." Reid tried to sound like he did this every day.

He had a little trouble getting in the elevator with their stuff. They got on first and then he followed. He decided to back in, with two bags under one arm and the fishing case in his other, straight up. When he was halfway in, the door started to close on him. Michelle jumped over and stuck out her hand to stop it.

"Thanks." *Another great impression. Bellhop gets squished in elevator door.* He put his head back and looked up at the numbers over the door, hoping she'd look up, too, the way people did in elevators, so she wouldn't see him blushing again.

They got off the elevator, and Reid trotted down the hall with the Lamonts' luggage with the Lamonts following behind. At least he knew where their room was, he thought as he opened the door to 426, and then tried to hide his surprise when he saw it. Jim Goltz had showed Reid and Abby one of the rooms when he gave them a tour of the lodge, but it had just been one of the regular rooms. Reid had thought *it* was unreal, but this was not to be believed.

The room looked like a fancy house. It was actually a suite; two bedrooms, two bathrooms, and a huge living room and dining area on the top floor of the lodge with a deck over-looking the marina. One of the bathrooms was bigger than Reid's entire studio apartment in the employee building.

"Just call the front desk if you need anything," Reid mum-bled, turning to leave. "Oh, sorry. I almost forgot."

He went to the cabinet, a beautifully carved yellow cedar armoire, and opened it. "Uh, there's videos for the VCR at the front desk."

Then he fumbled with the keys Jim had given him and went to the full bar at the end of the living room. "This is the refrigerator." He opened it, displaying the drinks and fancy nuts and snacks. "I'll leave the key here," he mumbled again, set-ting it on the bar as he turned to leave.

"Just a minute, Reid." Mr. Lamont walked toward him.

Oh, no! What'd I forget?

"Here you go." Mr. Lamont held out a bill. "Thanks."

"Oh, okay. Thank you very much, sir." Reid closed the door behind him and looked at the bill the guy had given him. Five bucks. Wow! Maybe Brad Wellman would have the flu for a long time and he could just do this bellhop job. He liked it much better than working with lettuce.

As he was getting off the elevator, Jim called to him, mo-tioning for him to come over to the desk. *Oh no. They've re-ported me already. Of course this was too good to be true.*

"Did the Lamonts get settled in okay?"

"Seemed to, they didn't ask me for anything."

"Good." Jim lowered his voice. "Reid, you may hear some folks talking about Lamont, he's a bit controversial. Robert La-mont is an executive with McMullen Blundeel."

Reid had never heard the name McMullen Blundeel spo-ken by his mother or any of her friends without her adding the phrase "those greedy butchers." It was like one word to her, as if the entire phrase were the actual company name: McMullen Blundeel Those Greedy Butchers. His whole life he'd been raised with the idea that these people were the enemy; but since he had never actually seen a timber company executive, it surprised him that Mr. Lamont looked like just a regular rich guy like you'd see on TV. There were no fangs or horns or anything to show he was one of the evil bad guys.

"We're in the service industry, and the lodge exists to provide service to the guests whether we approve of their line of work or their politics or anything else. I just wanted to make that clear."

"Okay, I won't poison them, ha-ha!" Reid laughed.

"No jokes, son."

"Sorry."

"That's okay. But since you're new, I wanted to remind you of our mission here."

On his way back to his apartment, Reid ran into Gloria. She was carrying a clothes basket, heading toward the employee laundry room.

"Want a hand with that?"

"It's not heavy."

"I need the practice," he put his hands on the basket. "I wasn't so great first time out as a bellhop."

"Okay, but I don't tip." She handed him the basket.

In the laundry room, Reid sat on one of the tables while Gloria put her clothes in the washing machine.

"How'd it go with your mum this morning?"

"She lives in a nice place. She was all settled and everything."

"You didn't have to unload all her stuff like you thought you would?" Gloria poured soap into the machine and closed the lid.

"She and that guy Harvey had it all done."

"You don't like him?"

"I didn't say that." Reid picked up her empty basket.

"Yeah, but your tone did and you scrunched up your mouth when you said his name."

"I did?" Reid felt his mouth with his hand. "I didn't know I did that."

"Yeah, when you don't like something, your mouth scrunches up at the corners. I've noticed this."

"Well, I'm not saying I don't like him, it's just that I was surprised. That's all. She's all set there, her place looks like she's been there forever, and she's joined some group called Bear Alert."

"Cool. My brother John's in that." Gloria walked over to the Coke machine next to the dryers, put in a loony, the one dollar coin, and took out a diet Coke. "He and this Chinese Canadian guy, Jeffrey Eng, do the educational stuff in the Asian communities."

"I just don't know if she understands what she's getting into, trying to stop poachers and trophy hunters. I mean, my mother sometimes just jumps into stuff."

"Look, it's true, the poachers are real scum. They're usually involved in drugs and weapons trafficking, too. But I've been to a couple of meetings with John and they're careful. People in Bear Alert wouldn't go out alone to intercept these guys." Gloria looked up at the clock on the wall over the dryers. "I better get over to the kitchen. I'll put my stuff in the dryer when I get my first break."

"Are you prepping again tonight?"

"It's me and the potatoes. And you?"

"Bussing tables."

"Good luck," she grinned.

"Is it hard?"

"No. As long as you don't listen to what the guests are saying and just try and focus on your job, it's okay."

When they got to the kitchen, Claude gave Reid a quick briefing on bussing the tables. "The server will offer them drinks, then you go to the table to fill the water glasses. Always lift the water glass away from the table to fill it. Fill it whenever it gets less than half-full. Serve from the left, take away from the right. Clear the plates as soon as the plate is empty and the guest has put the fork down. If the plate has food on it, but the fork has been put down, be sure and ask if you may clear the plate before you take it away. Bring the bread and olive oil as soon as the guests have placed their order with their server, and if the wine glasses need refilling, be sure and find their server to take care of it."

"Got it." Reid nodded and left for the dining room. This should be pretty easy, he thought. A lot better than having to cut up all those vegetables and jump in and out of the walk-in fridge to get stuff that he wasn't even sure what it was. Just fill the water, give 'em the bread, and take their plates when they're done. A piece of cake. Nothing to it.

In the dining room he stood next to the long sideboard, surveying the room. Pale yellow flowers in small crystal vases, gleaming silverware, and flickering candles were on every table. The room had a gentle radiance that contrasted sharply with the world just outside its wide expanse of glass; the sea, the storm-tossed driftwood, and the deep green of the enormous, ancient trees.

While he waited for guests to arrive, Reid thought about the beautiful girl in Room 426. He was sure that she and her father would have room service; they'd undoubtedly eat in their suite's private dining area, not here with the regular guests.

Maybe he could stick a little note on the cart that would be wheeled into their suite. It would be propped up next to the flowers, with her name on it. Michelle. A beautiful name. Wonder whether she has two *l*s or one? Probably two. A girl like that would have more of everything. He would write her name very nicely on the envelope of the card. Michelle. Then inside it would say something simple and right to the point. *For a good time, see Reid. Apt. #3.*

She would slip the card carefully into her pocket while her

father was in the bathroom or something, and then after the dining room closed and he was hanging out in his apartment he would hear this light tap-tap on his door.

"Reid, I came as soon as I could."

"Cool."

"Great apartment. Can I come in?"

"Be my guest."

"Do you live here alone?"

"Yes. We are alone, Michelle."

"Oh, Reid!" Then she throws herself into his arms and they kiss wildly, and passionately. "Oh, Reid. You are an animal!" She pants breathlessly. Then she takes his hand and . . .

Reid couldn't believe it. Michelle and her father walked into the dining room and Joan, the hostess, showed them to a corner table next to the window. He stared at them as they studied their menus, then Susan, their server, went to their table. *Susan's taking their drink orders. Okay, as soon as she leaves it's time for the water. Just pick up the glass, lift it away from the table, then replace it. Piece of cake. Nothing to it.* Reid watched the table carefully. *Okay, Susan's leaving to get their drinks, now go. Simple. Nothing to it. Serve from the left, take away from the right. Pick up glass, lift away from the table, fill, and replace.*

Reid grabbed a large water pitcher from the sideboard, then paused a minute. He held his shoulders back and lifted up his head. Pick up glass, lift away from the table, fill, and replace. Pick up glass, lift away from the table, fill, and replace. Pick up glass, lift away from the table, fill, and replace. He repeated it like a mantra as he crossed the dining room and walked toward their table, carefully holding the pitcher with two hands. Two more steps and he'd be there. *Pick up glass . . .*

"Hi, Reid." Michelle looked up at him and smiled. Her full lips parted, her teeth gleamed with their toothpaste advertisement whiteness, her cat's eyes shone and sparkled in the candlelight, her thick honey-blond hair hung softly around her shoulders.

"Hi, Michelle." He lifted the glass away from the table and returned her smile. Gazing and smiling into her lovely face, he poured the water. As he smiled, the water missed the glass and dumped all over her.

"Eeeeek!" she shrieked as some ice cubes bounced in her lap and water soaked her shoe.

"Oops! Sorry!" Reid set the pitcher on the table and bent to pick up the ice cubes from the floor. Mr. Lamont pulled his chair back.

"Are you out to get us, kid?" Mr. Lamont laughed and handed Michelle his napkin.

Reid crawled under the table trying to get more ice cubes. *He's gotta be there thinking, stay away from my daughter, you pervert. I didn't bring her to this place to have her spilled on by a clumsy, sex-starved maniac like you.*

"Sorry sir," Reid mumbled from under the table as Susan came up with their drinks.

"Reid," Susan leaned over and spoke to him in whisper, "just leave the ice cubes where they are. There are other guests now that need water."

"I've got almost all of them." His butt stuck out from under the tablecloth.

"Get out from under the table, Reid." Then she looked at Mr. Lamont. "I'm so sorry. Reid is new here."

"Surely you jest," Mr. Lamont said sarcastically, as Reid crawled out, bumping his head.

He wanted to slink right out of the dining room and right out of the lodge. But luckily for him, the worst was over; the Lamonts didn't drink much water so he didn't have to return to their table to fill their glasses again, just to get their plates.

He was still mortified, but as the evening wore on, he realized he had begun to get the hang of bussing. Not that he was perfect. There was the lady's fork that slipped off her plate as he was clearing it and stabbed her in the leg, and the man whose uneaten tomato flew into his lap as his salad plate was taken away. But all in all, Reid thought he had done a reasonably decent job.

When he did have to go back to the Lamonts' table, he pretended they were statues and that he was a robot automatically taking their plates away. Michelle looked out the window each time he came to the table so he didn't have to worry about her talking to him and messing up his concentration. But it also meant, without a doubt, that she thought he was a total jerk. And he felt like it, too. A complete jerk for imagining all that stuff about him and her together. What a laugh.

After the last guests had gone and the dining room was empty, Reid got his dinner from Claude and took it into the dining room where the staff was eating. On his way to the staff table, Susan took him aside and told him *never* to crawl around on the floor to clean up any dropped food. She reminded him that ice cubes also came in this category. "The items that should be picked and replaced are any silverware that falls or dishes or glasses."

"Okay."

"Just wanted to make sure you learned from this tonight, Reid," she said as she went back into the kitchen.

"Okay, I won't crawl under the tables again."

Gloria overheard him as she came out of the kitchen. "What was that about?"

They walked to the staff table and sat next to each other. "This looks great." Reid dug his fork into the pasta puttanesca Claude made for the staff.

"It is. Even though we don't get to eat the food from the menu, whatever he whips up for us is always fantastic." Gloria put her napkin on her lap. "So what were you telling Susan about the tables?"

"Susan?" Reid slurped the pasta.

"Yeah, Susan the server, just now. Look if you don't want to tell me . . ."

"It's just embarrassing, that's all."

"Everyone who works here has done something goofy. You can't help it. Stuff happens."

"I suppose so. Well, I dumped water on this girl, that's all."

"Oh."

"Then I crawled around under the table trying to get the ice cubes."

Gloria swallowed hard, like she was trying not to laugh. "Was it Lamont's daughter? She's the only guest I know about who's under the age of twenty."

"That's who it was."

"Well, I think she deserved it. You should have dumped the whole pitcher on her head and his, too. He's one of the top people who's responsible for the clear-cutting. They're destroying the old-growth forest."

"But she's not."

"Maybe in your heart you wanted to make sort of a statement. I don't mean exactly a planned thing. Maybe just a little protest that slipped out accidentally, since after all you'd been at the protests in ninety-three."

"No, I know it wasn't that."

"You were there, weren't you? I thought you told me that you and your mother were there. John and I were there with our parents."

"I was there, but I'm sure that's not the reason." Reid looked at Gloria and wondered if he should tell her. She had said that brother-sister stuff and he was sure now that meant she just wanted to be friends. And she seemed to want him to confide in her, like a friend would. Reid gulped. "See, it's just that she's so beautiful that I got sort of shook up."

Gloria picked up her plate. "I'm taking this back to my room to finish."

"You're leaving?"

"I'm tired," she said, coldly. "Bye, Reid."

"What's wrong?"

Gloria stomped back to the table. "You should have changed your name to Ken," she hissed.

"Ken?"

"It fits with Barbie!"

Reid watched her leave the dining room and then stared glumly at his plate, poking the pasta with his fork.

Chapter Eight

Reid got up early to work on his geometry assignment, hoping to get a lot of it done before he had to prep all the fresh fruit for the breakfast buffet. The assignment had to be in the mail by Wednesday. After twenty minutes of diameters, circumferences, and measuring a bunch of angles, his yawns became more and more frequent and the geometry got more and more boring. Better get some fresh air or this will never get done, he thought, stretching and yawning for the third time in two minutes.

He pulled on his sweatshirt and left the apartment, taking the path to the bluff southeast of the marina. The wooden bench there was one of his favorite spots on the island. Good. It's empty. Reid sat down, draping his arms over the back of the bench, stretching his legs out in front of him. He breathed in the crisp sea air, wishing he could sit there all morning and not have to finish his geometry and go cut up fruit. It was a good place to think. And there was plenty to think about, with his performance last night; dumping water on Michelle. And then Gloria all mad at him. Did she really expect him to do something like that on purpose just because Michelle's father was a lumber executive? It's not a person's fault who their parents are. Gloria had seemed so much more reasonable than that. And it was just a fact Michelle Lamont was beautiful. Anyone could see that, it's not like he confessed to Gloria all the stuff he'd been imagining.

Reid sat forward on the bench. Gloria was down on the dock. What was she doing down there? Then he remembered. It was Monday. The boat from the Opitsat village picked her up on its way to Tofino. Then the bus took them to Ukee. If he didn't get down there and talk to her, he wouldn't have another chance until she came back on Friday. He sat there, trying to get up his nerve.

Look, Gloria, I'm sorry I didn't dump the water on Michelle's head on purpose. Maybe I'm not as committed to saving the environment as you'd like me to be, but is that any reason to get so mad?

Or maybe he should just try to be cool and blow the whole thing off. *Hey, Gloria, I know there's no way you can stay mad at me. See you Friday, eh, sis?*

Reid sighed and kicked a stone next to the bench.

Why don't they teach you something useful in school, like How to Talk to Girls, instead of geometry, which is no help with anything in my life. *This is pathetic.*

Oh no, here comes the boat. It's now or never, he thought and sprang from the bench, charging along the path toward the steps, which he took two at a time.

"Gloria!"

He sprinted along the dock. Ahead of him a bunch of seagulls had been flocking around some fish guts that hadn't been completely cleaned off the dock, and the planks were slick with bird droppings.

"Hey, Gloria! Wait!"

As the boat pulled into the dock, he knocked over a bucket that had been left near one of the pilings. *Splat!* Fish guts all over the place. *Splat!* Reid slid on the slime. His legs flew out from under him. *Splat!*

As he landed on his butt, he could see the kids from the Opitsat village leaning over the rail, doubled up with laughter. Then Gloria waved and climbed aboard.

Fine. Laugh your heads off. Flattened by fish guts. Hilarious. He could hear them laughing as the boat left the dock and still laughing as it went down the channel on its way to their school bus in Tofino. Mustering as much dignity as he could, Reid picked himself up off the dock, wishing he was invisible. But as much as he wanted to be invisible, what he really wished was that he was on that boat.

As he was washing his hands at the faucet next to the steps, he saw an old fishing boat come down the channel. It was towing a smaller boat behind it, a skiff. Seemed like an odd combination. The fishing boat was gun-metal gray and pretty beat up. Neither boat looked like it would belong to guests that used this marina, that was for sure. Maybe some new employees.

Reid watched the boat go into a slip at the far end of the marina. A woman jumped out and secured the lines, then a guy handed her a large box. Then the guy jumped on the dock and tried to take the box away. He seemed to want to carry it for her and they horsed around, tugging it back and forth. Then the guy got it away from her. But he set it right down on the dock. Then he took her into his arms and kissed her. Just like that. Right there on the dock.

Reid thought about how he'd poured water on Michelle's foot and then about Gloria leaving without speaking to him. How come it's so easy for some people? He shut off the faucet and went up the stairs.

Behind him the laughter and voices of the couple from the old boats got louder as they got closer. In a second the voice became unmistakable; he didn't even need to turn around. His mother. His mother and Harvey, laughing and talking, her arm linked through his as Harvey carried the box for her and they came toward the stairs.

"Moonbeam!" She waved to him. "Hello!"

Reid went back down the steps and walked over to them. "Here, I'll take that." He grabbed the box from Harvey.

"It's okay, I've got it."

"I've got it." Reid yanked it away and rushed up the steps. Abby and Harvey followed behind him and he heard her whisper, "Shh, it's okay, Harv."

You're darn right it's okay, buddy. I've been taking care of stuff for her practically since I could walk. Reid waited at the top of the stairs. "You're taking this to the clothes shop, right?"

"Right. I'm meeting Anne Depue this morning. Keep your fingers crossed. Hopefully she'll want to sell some of my sweaters and shawls."

"Of course, she will. They're great." Reid walked ahead of them, clutching the box.

"That's what I've been telling her," Harvey chimed in.

Reid clutched the box tighter. *Shut up, mush mouth. Who asked you?* "I've got to get to work. I'll drop these off." Reid took off for the lodge, running as fast as he could.

He tore across the lobby and charged into the boutique. "Anne, hi!"

"Hi, Reid. What's the hurry?"

"Just brought this for Mum." He put the box on the counter. "She'll be here in a minute. Oh, by the way," he tried to sound casual, "I just wanted to mention that if she calls me this weird name, it's just a nickname she has for me. It's not my real name or anything."

Anne looked puzzled but before she could say anything he was out the door and halfway across the lobby. Abby and Harvey saw him as they came in the main door.

"I took the stuff to the shop," he told them.

"Thanks, Moonbeam." Abby smiled, not noticing him wince as she said his name. "Listen, Harvey's got a surprise for you. He can show you while I'm meeting with Anne."

So what. Who cares what he has. Reid headed for the door. "I've got to get to work pretty soon."

"It won't take long," Harvey assured him.

"I've got to be at work in twenty minutes."

"That's plenty of time." Harvey smiled. "All we need to do is go back down to the marina for a few minutes. Okay?"

"Okay. I guess so," he said, wishing the minute he said it that he had just said no.

"How do you like your job so far?" Harvey asked as they walked on the path leading to the marina.

Reid didn't say a word until they reached the steps.

"Okay." *It's none of your business, seagull slime.*

"Meeting some people your age? Your mum said she thought that would be a nice thing for you."

Not another word until the bottom of the steps.

"Some." *Don't tell me what my mum says, you jerkhead.*

"I noticed a hoop near the apartments. You play there?"

Nothing until they were at the south end of the marina. "A little." *Just show me your stupid surprise and shut up, maggot.*

"Well, here we are." Harvey stopped in front of the old fishing boat. Reid looked at the writing on the hull. CLAYOQUOT BIOSPHERE PROJECT. So that was it. This must be the boat he uses when he goes around the sound counting birds and fish or whatever it is he's doing.

"I'm going to be using the marina as a base. I'll be in and out of here a lot, but I'm not going to be using my skiff much so I thought I'd leave it here for you." Harvey pointed to the smaller boat, tied to the fishing boat.

"You mean for me to just use? Like whenever I want to?" *What are you trying to do, buy me off?*

"Sure. Abby says you've driven one like this before."

"On Sproat Lake. Rainbow Callanti's father used to fish there and we'd trailer his boat over from Heather Mountain." Reid walked over to the skiff and looked at the motor, then the steering wheel, the choke, and the throttle. "It's pretty much the same."

"Good." Harvey looked at him, like he was waiting for something.

Reid stared at the skiff. *If you think I'm going to roll over this easy, you're crazy.*

"It handles well. But I wouldn't take it out in anything too rough," Harvey advised.

"I wouldn't." *I know that, you idiot. What do you think I am, some fool that doesn't know the difference between a lake and an ocean?* "But I don't think I'd really use it."

"It's in good shape. You just have to supply the gas."

"I wasn't going to hit you up for gas money." Reid was insulted.

"That's not what I meant. I meant just that it's in good shape and ready to use," Harvey said patiently.

Reid put his hands in his pockets and looked down at the boat. *Just say it. It won't kill you. Even if he does have slimy ulterior motives, you gotta say it.*

"Yeah, well, thanks," he finally mumbled.

"Here's the keys." Harvey reached in his pocket and handed him a set of keys with a small float attached to the key ring.

Reid looked at the keys, then he looked at Harvey. "I'm not going to need those."

The words just came out of his mouth, surprising him almost as much as Harvey, but he didn't seem to be able to stop them. He just couldn't stand the idea of taking anything from this guy. He didn't want to owe him any more than he already did for helping him get the job in the first place. Harvey Hattenbach had moved in on their lives too much as it was. Maybe the guy could take over with his mother, but he'd better think twice if he thought all he had to do was bribe him with his stupid boat. Besides, the way things were going, he was sure he couldn't get anyone to go boating with him anyway.

"Thanks anyway," Reid muttered. Then he turned and walked back to the lodge, leaving Harvey standing on the dock next to his boats.

Abby met him on the path as she was leaving the lodge. She seemed to be in a hurry.

"Honestly, I don't know how you can stand it." She balanced the box on her knee.

"Stand what, Mum?"

"The people in this place. The sooner I get back to Palmer's Land the better." Abby ran her hand through her hair, and looked back at the lodge. "I knew it would be like this."

"I thought you liked Anne Depue."

"Not her. She's lovely. There was this young girl in the shop, one of the guests. She came over to look at what I was showing Anne and Anne tells her they're handwoven and that I spin the wool myself and the girl says, 'how sweet.' Then she says how her mother says we should encourage cottage industries, but of course her mother only buys Missoni knits. Then she prances out of the shop."

"I don't really get it." Reid looked at his watch.

"Go ahead. I know you have to go to work." She kissed him on the cheek. "I don't expect you to get it. Missoni's a fancy Italian designer of knits and that girl was just an arrogant, patronizing little twit, that's all. I know her type like I know the back of my hand."

Reid walked backwards on the path. "Is the shop going to sell your stuff?"

"She took six out of eight!" Abby picked up the box.

"Not bad!" He waved, then turned and jogged toward kitchen.

"Hey!" She called after him. "What'd you think of Harvey's surprise?"

Reid kept jogging, hoping she'd think he hadn't heard.

Reid worked on his geometry between the lunch and dinner shift and by midmorning the next day he had finished not only all the assignments that were due, but even a few that weren't due for another three weeks. When he lived at Heather Mountain, Meadow's dad had explained everything really well. The work wasn't all that hard for him, just long and time-consuming, which was why he avoided it. But with Gloria gone this week, he was actually glad to have something to take his mind off things. He just wished Friday would get here so she would be back.

Reid didn't realize how much he had depended on talking to her. The other kids his age who were going to work here wouldn't start until school was out. Until then, Gloria was it. But even if there were lots of people his age at the lodge right now, he knew he'd still want to spend time with her. She was really nice. He just wished they could have talked before she left Monday.

Michelle was a whole other story. After the disaster in the dining room Sunday night, he had stopped daydreaming about her. A girl like that was just out of reach.

And as for Harvey and his mother. Well, they seemed perfectly happy to have him stuck out here on this island and out of their way. That was probably why Harvey brought the skiff. So he'd stay here on his days off and leave the love birds alone. Well, it hadn't worked. And on his next day off he was going to Palmer's Land and he'd hang around and get in their face and there would be nothing they could do about it. He'd also eat the blueberry jam. All of it.

After the lunch shift, he gave his assignments to Amy at the front desk to put with the rest of the mail that would go out later that afternoon. Then he got his basketball from his apartment and went to the court to shoot some hoops. Reid stood in the center of the court facing the basket, holding the ball at his side.

"Oh, Canada, our home and native land. True patriot's love, in all our sons command." The national anthem starts the game.

His first shot goes in. *Swish!* Beautiful. He gets the rebound, takes it out, pivots, then drives for the basket. Score! Fantastic. There's no stopping him.

"You're really good."

"Huh?" Reid swung around and the ball bounced out of his hands. He couldn't believe it. She was standing there. Right next to the court, watching him. Michelle Lamont, looking like a movie star or a model or something. She was chewing a blade of grass and leaning back against the trunk of one of the huge trees on the edge of the court.

The ball bounced several times, then rolled toward Michelle. She moved away from the tree, kneeled down, and picked it up. Then she walked slowly over to Reid.

"Here." Her voice was soft and breathy as she handed him the ball, and she stood very close to him, looking up at him with her cat eyes.

"Thanks," he stammered, taking the ball from her. Then he began nervously dribbling it in place, not sure what to do next.

"You must play on a team or something." She smiled her dazzling smile, still standing just inches from him.

"No, not really."

"Not at school?"

"No." He bounced the ball in place and looked at the ground.

"I would have bet anything you were a first-string starter."

"Really?" Reid gulped. Then he bounced the ball some more.

"Absolutely." She sighed. "You just looked fantastic, the way you shot and everything."

"Well, actually I did play a little at my other school." Reid began to dribble the ball toward the basket.

"What school?" Michele followed him along the side of the court.

"A school near Heather Mountain." He pivoted and shot.

"Oh, that was close," she said appreciatively as the ball bounced off the backboard.

Reid got the rebound and drove into the basket. His famous hook shot. This time it went in.

"Great!" she squealed, like his own private cheerleader. "I've heard of a prep school called Mountain Academy, is that where you played?"

"Yeah." The word just came out of his mouth. He didn't know how it happened.

"They must have won every time you played."

"Well, sort of."

"Are you working here while you're on spring break?"

"Not exactly." Reid caught the rebound and went straight up for his jump shot.

"Oh, almost," she said, as the ball hit the rim of the basket. "You must be on leave from school on one of those work-study practicums, right?"

"Yeah."

"Does it get kind of boring? It seems pretty quiet being stuck out here on this island away from everything."

"There's the usual outdoor stuff." Reid's next shot missed the basket, hit the backboard, then bounced toward her.

"I suppose that means hiking, fishing, hunting." Michelle ran after the ball, picked it up, and tossed it toward him. "You probably do all that stuff."

"Yeah." Reid had to lunge to get the ball, which missed him by three feet.

"Nice catch, bad throw." She laughed. "What do they hunt for around here?"

"Oh, the usual."

"Like deer and bear, I suppose."

"Yeah."

"When we flew in, we started coming down by this island not too far from here and the pilot pointed out a black bear that was sunning himself on a rock. It looked like it could kill someone just as easy as look at them. It was huge."

"They get pretty big," Reid said with authority.

"Is that the kind you hunt?" Michelle's eyes were wide.

"Oh, yeah," Reid said casually, while he dribbled the ball toward the basket.

"I'd love to go with you." She walked over under the basket and put her arms around the pole that held it.

"Huh?" Reid threw an air ball.

"We're only here for a week." She held on to the pole and leaned out next to him, swinging back and forth. "When's your day off?"

"Thursday."

"That's the day after tomorrow."

"Uh-huh."

"Great, we can go then!" Michelle smiled, tossing her head back. Then she let go of the pole and pranced off through the trees.

Reid watched her disappear down the path. Slowly he walked toward his apartment like he was dazed, or underwater, or in a dream. At his door, he fumbled with the handle like a sleepwalker, then shut it behind him, crossed the small room, and slumped on the couch.

He stared at the walls. How had this happened? Michelle Lamont thinks he's the star basketball player for some fancy prep school who's here on some kind of work-study deal and that he goes hunting all the time and that on Thursday he's going to take her bear hunting.

Bear hunting! He'd never held a gun in his life, much less gone hunting for animals. His mother had always been completely against guns. She had never let him have one, not even a toy gun. Not even a water pistol. What a mess! How was he ever going to get out of this?

Reid went in the bathroom and splashed cold water on his face. Could he just tell her the truth?

Michelle, I lied. I do not go to Mountain Academy. For five years I lived at the Happy Children of the Good Earth commune near Heather Mountain, and I don't own a gun, and not only that, I have no idea how to shoot one. I have never gone hunting in my life.

Reid splashed some more water on his face, then grabbed the towel and dried it. Then it hit him. Michelle Lamont had actually talked to him! She actually came over and hung around him!

Michelle, now that we've gotten everything out in the open, what I would like to do on my day off is go off into the forest with you or perhaps you would like to see my apartment. I have some activities in mind that I'm sure you would find much more won-

derful than hunting for bear, which I don't know anything about. (Actually I don't know a lot about these other activities either, but I'm sure I could get the hang of it.) So how 'bout it, Michelle? Shall we bag the bear hunt on Thursday and head straight for my apartment?

Chapter Nine

Reid was glad when Claude assigned him to dishwashing that night. He wouldn't have to worry about remembering the names of fancy food or dumping stuff on the guests. Washing dishes was so automatic, spray . . . swish . . . stack . . . spray . . . swish . . . stack, that he didn't even have to think about it. This was especially good since it gave him a chance to try and figure out something for getting out of the mess with Michelle.

Spray . . . swish . . . stack . . . spray . . . swish . . . stack. While the water steamed over the plates he made a mental list of what he thought his options were.

1. Avoid her and then hide somewhere on the island until his day off was over.
2. Tell her his gun was broken.
3. Tell her his hand was messed up and wrap it up with a bunch of Band-Aids.
4. Tell her he had the flu. She could stay in his apartment and take care of him.

But by the time he finished work that night, he still wasn't any farther along in making a plan than when he started. Discouraged, Reid said goodnight to Claude and left for his apartment. He just didn't feel like eating with the staff, and Claude said he could take his dinner with him.

Outside the kitchen, he leaned against the side of the building and ate the staff's dinner. Chicken curry. Yum. Claude had made it from the leftover herb-roasted chicken entree. The chilly night air felt great after so many hours of working in the steaming kitchen with the near-boiling spray of the water, and he decided to stay outside for a bit. The stars were brilliant in the clear black sky, and he could hear the sound of the masts clanging down below at the marina. Reid looked at the marina lights twinkling along the docks and all of a sudden he had his plan.

That's it! I don't have to actually *go* bear hunting. All I have to do is *pretend* to go bear hunting. It was so obvious. Why hadn't he thought of it before? Now, if only Harvey would still let him have that boat. Reid wolfed down the rest of the chicken curry, dropped his plate off in the kitchen, and ran down the path toward the marina. And now if only the boat's still there, Reid thought as he tore along the path. He said he'd be using the marina as a base, that'd he'd be in and out a lot.

All right! Luck was on his side. Reid spotted the old fishing boat right where it had been in the same slip! And even better than that, the skiff was there, too.

"Harvey!" Reid called as he ran alongside the boat. "Harvey, it's me!"

Harvey stuck his head out of the cabin. "You're sure in a hurry."

"I've got to talk to you."

"Come on board. Are you okay?" He held out his hand for Reid to grab as he jumped from the dock. "Careful, the light's not so great."

"Thanks." Reid jumped, ignoring the hand.

"We can talk in the cabin where it's warm."

"Okay." Reid ducked his head as he followed Harvey down the steps.

In the cabin, Harvey lit the stove, firing up a burner underneath the kettle. "Want some tea?"

"Sure, thanks." Reid sat at the table.

"So, what's the problem?" Harvey leaned back against the stove, waiting for the water to boil.

"There's nothing wrong. I mean, everything's okay. It's just that I decided to take you up on your offer of the boat. I mean, if it's still offered."

"Sure. The offer's still good."

"Great. See, I need it Thursday on my day off."

"There's plenty of gas so it's all ready to go."

Reid looked out the cabin window, trying to get up the nerve to make his next request. "Well, there's something else. And, um, I'm not sure how to explain it, exactly."

The kettle started to whistle. "Well," Harvey said calmly, taking the kettle off the burner, "maybe just try starting at the beginning."

"Okay."

"Sugar?" Harvey poured the water over the tea bags.

"Two lumps. Thanks."

He brought their tea to the table and sat across from Reid.

"See there's this girl I met here."

"Uh-huh."

"And we were just talking and then it just—"

Harvey stirred his tea. "Just talking and then what?"

"And now I'm taking her bear hunting."

"Bear hunting." Harvey sipped his tea. "With cameras I suppose, the way they take people out to photograph bears in Alaska."

"No. Real hunting. And I can't back out."

"Did she assume that you were a hunter?"

"Yeah, that was it. She starting making all these assumptions and I guess I just didn't get around to correcting her."

"That can happen." Harvey stroked his chin.

"And she thinks I'm taking her on my day off, and I didn't know how I was going to get out of it but then I thought maybe I could pull it off if I just pretended to go bear hunting."

"So you'd drive the boat around and maybe get out on one of the islands."

"Right." Reid took a sip of tea. "I'd walk around with a gun like I was hunting and then just get back in the boat after a while and that would be it."

"That should do it."

"Although she did see a bear on an island near here when she was flying in on Sunday. She probably wants to go to that island."

"If it's Hope Island, there's enough gas. It's just north of here." Harvey opened the cupboard and took out a chart and spread it out on the table.

"I don't know what I'd do if a bear did come out of the bushes."

"This is Hope." Harvey pointed on the chart to a small island between Vargas and Stubbs, due north of Stere. "About ten kilometers north."

"But what if we did see the bear?"

"That bear is more scared of you than you are of it. The bears on the uninhabited islands aren't like the ones near towns where they've learned about the dump. Where they associate people with food. On those little islands the bears are extremely shy."

"You really think this would work?" Reid drummed the top of the table with his fingertips.

"I don't see why not. She probably wouldn't know the gun wasn't loaded. You can use my .303. I have to go back to my place tomorrow and I can bring it out here tomorrow night and put it under the tarp of the skiff for you."

"You're sure it's no trouble?"

"No. Like I said, I'm going back tomorrow anyway."

"Is the .303 the gun that's near the back door at your place?"

"Yes. It's the only one I've got."

"You don't hunt, do you?"

"No. The only reason I got it was that last winter a cougar attacked a couple of my neighbors' dogs. One was killed and another one was messed up pretty bad. I wanted to be able to protect Gretta if one came around and I couldn't scare it away."

"My mother is against guns, completely."

"I agree with her in most cases. I never have understood people who get off on killing birds and animals, unless they need to eat."

"She's even against killing for food."

"I don't go that far, but if it weren't for that cougar I probably still wouldn't own a gun."

Reid stood up. "Guess I better get some sleep."

Harvey grabbed a set of keys from a hook next to the door. "Here you go." He handed Reid the keys.

"Thanks." Reid stuffed them in his pocket, then climbed out of the cabin.

Harvey followed him out on the deck. "Let me know if you need anything else."

"Thanks a lot." Reid jumped onto the dock. "Thanks for everything. Oh, Harvey?"

"Yeah?"

"I don't think we need to tell Mum about this, do you?"

Harvey smiled. "I don't think it's really necessary."

The guy's not so bad after all, Reid thought, tossing the keys up in the air and catching them. He opened the door to his apartment, flipped on the light, shut the door behind him, and went to the kitchen. There were a few Cokes in the refrigerator, and he grabbed one and took it to the bedroom.

Now that he had a bear hunting plan, Reid was filled with relief. He lay on his bed, drinking Coke and thinking about this bear hunting in great detail.

It's going to be so great. Michelle will stomp around at my side on that little island holding tightly to my free arm (the one that's not holding the gun) and after a little while it will get boring, because the shy bear won't get near us and then she'll want a little excitement and she'll think of some better stuff for us to do on that deserted little island out in the middle of nowhere. ALL RIGHT! YES!

Reid snapped off the light and tried to fall asleep thinking wonderful thoughts about him and Michelle on the island. But after a few minutes, he started to worry. He sat up in bed and put the light back on. What if Harvey was wrong? What if the bear wasn't shy at all and it attacked them and chased them back to the boat? (If it didn't catch them and rip them to shreds!) Then she'd see what a phony he was.

And he was phony, not only about that, but about Harvey, too. He'd been thinking all this rotten stuff about him, but then, when he's in desperate need of boat and a gun, all of a sudden, old Harv isn't so bad. Reid's brain felt scrambled. The boat and the gun couldn't change the fact that he didn't like the way the guy was all over his mother out on the dock the morning that Gloria left. Gloria! Oh, no. What if Gloria found out about this bear hunt? She'd really hate him.

Reid shut off the light and threw himself back on the bed. His brain felt fried. He closed his eyes and began counting sheep.

The next day, Reid went down to the marina as soon as he was through work. When he thought about it, he had to admit that it had been a little while since he had driven Rainbow's dad's boat on Sproat Lake. He thought driving a boat was probably just like riding a bike, the kind of thing you always remember how to do. But just to make sure, he decided it would be good to take Harvey's skiff for a spin. Better get a little practice. Then he'd have real experience handling the boat and there'd be one less thing to feel phony about.

As he walked down the steps to the marina, he looked over to the far end where Harvey's boat was moored. The biosphere project boat was gone! What if Harvey forgot to leave the skiff, or left the skiff but hadn't gone this morning to get the gun like he promised? What if he was a jerk after all? Someone who never came through and just told people what they wanted to hear. What if he'd told his mother and then she flipped out, and to get in good with her Harvey decided to forget the whole thing?

Reid got more and more worried as he ran the length of the dock. An enormous yacht had arrived and was moored in front of Harvey's slip, blocking everything from view. It must have come in late last night, or early this morning. Reid held his breath running past the yacht and didn't let it out until he was beyond its stern and saw Harvey's skiff. Whew! At least it was still there.

Carefully, he unhooked the tarp. Pulling it back, he climbed into the boat, then crouched by the steering wheel and stuck his head under the bow. An olive green tarp was folded in half, covering most of the deck under the bow. Reid lifted it up and peeked under the top fold. It was there! A man of his word, that Harvey. The dark brown handle of the .303 nestled in the folds of the tarp. Reid touched the handle, then ran his hand along the barrel. *Guns are for killing and killing is wrong!* He could hear his mother's voice as he touched the rifle and he suddenly felt like a criminal.

The evil of guns had been drummed into his head ever since he could remember and it was hard to feel relaxed about this whole thing. His mother treasured the fact that Canada, her adopted homeland, had a minuscule number of murders compared to the States, and she never lost an opportunity to use the States as an example of how things ran amok when people could easily get guns. Just looking at the gun spooked him. Even if it wasn't loaded. Even if it was just a fake bear hunt.

And it wasn't just guns. Abby Dawson was dead set against anything that even hinted at violence. If it hadn't been for that guy Gregory Thomas that she hung around with when they lived in Victoria, he wouldn't have even been allowed to play peewee hockey. Gregory Thomas told her that if young males were allowed to glide around on ice skates and bash each other with wooden sticks in an organized setting, they would see this as the proper way to discharge their aggression and would be more peaceful when they got to be adults. So she finally signed the peewee hockey permission slip in the interest of his growing up to be a peaceful adult.

Reid looked at the rifle as if it were a poisonous snake. He covered it up again with the tarp, reminding himself that the thing wasn't loaded and all he was going to do was carry it around a bit. Nothing deadly about that, he thought, as he slid into the seat in front of the steering wheel. He pulled the keys out of his pocket and slipped the key in the ignition. Oops. Got to pull out the choke. Almost forgot that. It's a good thing I'm having a practice run here, he thought as he put the gear in neutral, pulled out the choke, and turned the key. The engine caught right away. Reid let it idle in neutral as he pulled in the bumpers, uncleated the lines, and then pushed off from the dock. He put it in forward gear and gently pushed on the throttle, cautiously steering the skiff around the huge yacht. Big gold letters heralded its name across the stern, *Regina II*. And below that, in smaller letters, its home port, VANCOUVER, B.C. That's some big hunk of fiberglass; probably could belong to a queen, he thought, as he eased around it.

The wind picked up when he drove outside the channel marker. Reid pushed on the throttle and the boat moved ahead with a burst of speed, its bow high in the air for a few minutes before it started to plane. Picks up great. Reid grinned, feeling the saltwater spray on his face and the wind in his hair. He couldn't think of a single time that he'd ever driven alone. He'd always been with Rainbow or with Rainbow and his dad. He saw the whole ocean ahead of him and he began turning the boat, steering it in huge circle eights. "YE-OOW!" He let out a joyous yelp knowing that only the seagulls overhead could hear him. Incredible. There wasn't a person in sight. It was like a rush. Freedom!

He pulled the throttle back, slowing the boat, and took two more big swings driving in large circles, turning first to the east and then to the west before he reluctantly turned back and headed for the marina.

At the dock he checked out the anchor to make sure the lines were secure, since he thought he and Michelle would probably anchor next to a steep bank tomorrow. Most of those islands had sharp drop-offs, which was good because you didn't have to worry about shearing a pin if you went in too shallow and didn't pull the skiff up in time. Good. This stuff had all come back to him, Reid thought as he put the bumpers out, tied the lines, and pulled the tarp over the boat. Just like riding a bike.

When he got back to the marina, Michelle was waiting at the top of the steps. She smiled and waved to him as he started up the stairs.

"Were you just out in your boat?" she asked in her soft breathy voice.

"Hi." Reid walked up the steps, feeling like he owned the place, enjoying the fact that she had seen him drive in. "Yeah, I just got here."

"Is that the boat we'll take hunting?" She walked along next to him.

"That's the one. I was just checking a few things out."

"My dad's friend came in last night on the *Regina II*. It's the boat right next to yours. They're going fishing early tomorrow."

"It's a good idea to start early if you want those chinooks," Reid said, trying to sound like an expert.

"Do you have to go early to hunt, too?"

"Oh sure," he said, casually.

"What time?"

"Dawn. The bear's more likely to be moving around then."

"Oh, well where should I meet you?" Michelle put her hand on his arm and gazed eagerly at him with her gold-and-green cat's eyes.

At my apartment. Then you can come in and we can bag this whole dumb hunting thing.

"Down at the dock."

"What time exactly?"

"When does your dad leave?"

"I think he told Mr. Roessler that he'd be down there at five-thirty."

"Okay, I'll meet you at six." Reid looked at his watch. "Well, I've got to go and get ready for the next shift."

"See you later," she started to leave, then hesitated a minute and turned back. "Reid, I just can't wait until tomorrow. I'm really excited about this."

"Yeah, well." Reid gulped, grinning nervously. "See you in the morning."

Chapter Ten

Reid's alarm went off at 5:30. He grabbed the clock and went to the window and opened the drapes. It was still kind of dark out. Maybe the bear on that island would decide that it was too early to get up and it would just go back to the cave and sleep some more.

Reid dressed quickly and then quietly slipped out of his apartment. He couldn't believe he was actually doing this, taking a beautiful girl out in a boat to an island in the middle of nowhere. Just a couple of weeks ago he was living at the Happy Children of the Good Earth commune, hanging out with Meadow MacLaine and wishing there were some girls his age. What a change! And Michelle Lamont wasn't just any girl. She was so beautiful and sophisticated, he didn't know girls like her existed. And here she was, wanting to be with him. Amazing.

Down at the dock Reid pulled the tarp off Harvey's boat, folded it, and put it under the bow. Then he took the rifle from between the folds of the smaller tarp and held it for a few minutes, trying to get comfortable holding the thing, although he doubted that could every really be possible. He tried picking it up and setting it down a few times as if grabbing the gun from under the bow was something he'd been doing for years. Then he picked it up and turned toward the channel marker, planted his feet firmly, and aimed the gun at the red buoy. He felt his knees go weak and was sure that any minute the sky would open and an Angel of Peace would swoop down and let him have it. *What's wrong with you, jerkhead! Put that gun down. Who do you think you are? You weren't raised to mess with guns! If you go over to the other side the whole world will get out of balance, the voices of reason will lose the fight and the whole universe will blow up in your face, you snail brain!*

Then there would be a huge roar of thunder and a crack of lightning and the Angel of Peace would konk him on the head with a bolt of lightning. *Take that, you rodent!*

The gun would fly out of his hands. Burned to a crisp. Michelle would come, laugh in his face, and that would be the end of everything.

Reid turned around and put the rifle back under the bow, placing it carefully on top of the tarps so Michelle would be sure and see it. He jumped out on the dock and then looked back under the bow, trying to get used to the idea of the thing lying there. He sure hoped that when the time came to pick it up and carry it around that he wouldn't be bothered by any voices from the sky waiting up there to zap him.

Reid sighed and leaned against the pilings near the skiff, waiting for her to come. He looked at his watch, 6 A.M. on the dot. He glanced at the rifle lying on the tarp under the bow and was glad he'd gotten down a few minutes early. At least he'd picked the thing up a few times.

The sun was just beginning to come up and the huge cedars looked black against the blue gray of the early morning sky. Up at the lodge, the lights were coming on as the kitchen staff was prepping for breakfast and the guests were getting up to go fishing. Reid saw that the *Regina II* had gone, which meant that Michelle's father had gotten the early start he'd planned.

Reid hadn't thought too much about Michelle's family situation before, but while he waited for her he began to wonder why they hadn't come with her mother. It seemed kind of strange that a guy would take his daughter on a vacation during spring break and that the mother wouldn't come. Then he wondered if maybe she didn't have a mother. Probably divorced. But maybe her mother was dead, just like his father was dead. Maybe she never knew her mother either and they had this whole thing in common. Being an only child and having just one parent with the other one dead. The more he thought about it, the more Reid was sure this might really be the case. That they had this whole bond with their family situations even though her dad was a timber executive and his mum hated logging.

The air was chilly and Reid pulled his collar up around his neck. The sky was lighter now, and the cedar trees took on a deep green as dawn began to break. A small figure made its way down the path from the lodge toward the marina steps. Reid's heart fired like a machine gun as he recognized Michelle. Her hair was fastened back and she wore a cream-colored fisherman's sweater and jeans. She waved from the top of the steps and Reid waved back.

He climbed in the boat and put the keys in the ignition and then checked the gas tank. Good old Harv. It was full. He must have stopped by last night to check on it, and then filled it. Reid hopped out of the boat and walked to meet Michelle as she came down the dock. If only Meadow MacLaine could see him now.

"This is sure early." She yawned. "I almost went back to sleep after the alarm went off."

"It's part of what you've got to do if you want to hunt." Reid tried to act like he did this every day.

"That's what my dad says about fishing." She looked at the slip where the *Regina II* had been moored. "Guess he got off all right."

"They were gone by the time I got down here." Reid led the way to the boat and pulled it in close to the dock.

"This is really small." She frowned as she looked at the skiff.

Reid laughed. "Especially if you're only used to things the size of that boat your dad's on." Reid hopped in then held out his hand for her.

"Are you sure it's safe and everything?" she asked, grabbing his hand.

"Sure. It's really calm out there this morning." As he helped her into the boat, Reid noticed that her nails were polished perfectly, each one a bright pink oval, like she was going to a party or something. He put his arm around her waist to steady her as she carefully stepped first on the deck and then on the driver's seat.

"I just haven't been on a boat this teensy." She laughed as the boat rocked.

"Just sit here in the driver's seat and hold the dock while I untie us. Then you can sit next to me when we get underway."

Michelle sat down and clutched the edge of the dock. "Oooh, it's rough." She drew one of her hands back. "I hope I don't get splinters."

"Just hold tight, we're almost ready to fend off. I'm done with the stern." Reid ran to the bow and uncleated the line. "Okay, you can scoot over now."

Michelle let go of the dock and moved over as Reid jumped in the driver's seat. He held the dock with one hand while he started the engine. "Forgot the bumpers, can you hold on again?"

"I guess so." Michelle didn't seem too pleased, but she got in the driver's seat and grabbed the dock again while he pulled up the bumper from the stern.

"Okay, just one more minute while I get it from the bow." He climbed over the windshield and flipped the bumper into the boat. Michelle moved next to him as he got back in the driver's seat.

Reid put the boat in gear, steering carefully away from the dock while Michelle examined her fingernails. The dawn had broken and the sky and the ocean took on a rosy glow as he drove slowly through the channel.

After a minute she looked up. "It's really pretty out here."

"I love it early like this."

"My dad does, too." She yawned. "But I'd usually rather sleep in."

Reid decided this might be a good time to ask about her family. "What about your mum?"

"Oh, she hates fishing."

"Is that why she didn't come?"

"No. They're divorced. And he gets me on my spring break. We always have to do what he wants, and it's usually fishing on one of his friend's boats, which I find totally boring."

"So you must be an only child." Reid steered carefully next to the channel marker. "That's what I am."

"No, my mother had a kid with her second husband. Ashley, my half sister, goes to Hawaii spring break with her dad, which is a much better deal than having to go salmon fishing. My mother's in the sun, too. She and Pete, her third husband, are in Palm Springs."

"But they don't get to go bear hunting where they are."

Michelle laughed. "This year I put up such a fuss about having to be stuck on a boat the whole time that my dad said we could come here. Sort of a compromise. But it's still boring." Michelle shivered and leaned close to him. "Jeez, it's cold out here."

Reid decided this must mean he was supposed to put his arm around her, so he did. She cuddled next to him and she was so casual about it, he figured getting close to guys was probably an everyday kind of thing with her. Then today was his lucky day. That was for sure.

"How long does it take to get to the island?"

"About twenty minutes, if we go full speed." Reid reached for the throttle. "Want to?"

"Sure."

Michelle's eyes got wide as he thrust the throttle hard and the boat shot across the waves. She leaned even closer to him, and her body pressed against him with every bounce of the boat. She said something, but he couldn't hear her over the motor. He slowed the boat down.

"Couldn't hear you."

She glanced at the rifle under the bow. "If we get the bear, how do we get him back to the resort?"

"I've got a friend with a converted fishing boat. We'll come back and haul it out." Reid thrust the throttle forward and she leaned against him again as the boat went full speed. They couldn't talk over the roar of the engine, which was fine with him. That way she couldn't ask any more bear hunting questions and he wouldn't have to make up more stuff, and he especially liked the way they were squished together with her pressing into him with every bounce of the boat. Boating with Meadow MacLaine was never like this!

"Reid, look!" Michelle sat up and pointed to something off the bow.

He pulled back on the throttle, slowing the boat. "What is it?"

"There! See, that speck over to the left? I think it's the island."

Reid turned the boat toward the speck and then picked up speed a bit. "Does this look like the place where you saw the bear?"

"It's hard to tell, it looked different from the plane. But it wasn't a little dinky island or anything and this one looks fairly big."

"This is Hope Island," Reid said, remembering what Harvey had told him. "It's about three kilometers long and about one and a half across."

Reid brought the boat in close to the shore and began circling the island, looking for a good place to beach the boat. The island was empty except for some seagulls hanging out on the rocks. So far so good. He pulled back the throttle to almost an idle so that they just inched along a few feet from the rocky shore.

"Can you imagine owning this island and putting a fantastic house on it and having this whole place to yourself?" Michelle looked up into the huge trees that came practically down to the water.

"It might get kind of lonely."

"Just to come on weekends when you felt like it. You'd have a plane to go back and forth to Vancouver, naturally." Michelle looked up at him. "Where do you live, anyway?"

"I went to school near Heather Mountain."

"I mean when you're not at school. Where does your family live?"

Reid steered the boat farther out, away from some rocks that jutted out from the bank. "It's just me and my mum. She lives in Tofino."

"My dad said that's where all the granolas and the tree huggers live." Michelle laughed. "But he says that it's changing and that there are some beautiful big homes on some of the beaches. Retired executives and people like that, not just hippies anymore."

"There sure doesn't seem to be anything here." Reid changed the subject as he rounded the rocky point and turned back in closer to shore.

"If you were a bear I bet this would be a great place to live."

"I suppose so." He looked up into the trees, hoping not to see anything except trees.

"Sure, especially if there was a honey tree like Pooh had," she giggled and snuggled next to him. "Ashley, my little half sister that I was telling you about, she loves bears. She has a whole collection of teddy bears. Over a hundred of them, from all over the world."

"I had a nice Pooh when I was little." He held her close to him, steering easily with his right hand, enjoying the slow rocking of the boat as they inched along.

"Me, too. And I had a book about Paddington. I got it when we were in London, a first edition."

Reid smiled. "I liked Smokey the Bear a lot."

"I thought Yogi Bear was great." She put her head on his shoulder.

Slowly, Reid steered the boat around the east side of the island. The rocks jutted out into the water and he hoped he wasn't getting in too close. The last thing he needed was to shear a pin.

"Oh!" Michelle shrieked and sat straight up, clutching the dashboard.

Reid thought he was going to pass out when he saw it. A huge black bear ambled through the brush, crashing everything in its path with its huge bulk. It sounded like an enormous tank was coming toward them. At the water's edge the bear stopped, turned, and stared at them.

They were only a few meters from the gigantic black furry mass, and they could hear it breathing with breath that sounded like great gusts of wind as it rustled the leaves on the undergrowth at the water's edge. The bear froze, staring at them, and they stared back at the bear. Then after a minute, as if coming out of a trance, Michelle looked under the bow at the .303 and grabbed Reid's arm. "Reid! Don't get the gun. Don't! I can't let you. Think of Pooh . . . and Paddington . . . and Smokey." She held his arm and looked up at him, pleading with her beautiful cat's eyes. "Don't do it, Reid. Please!"

"Okay," he gasped, "I won't shoot him." Reid pulled her close to him and hit the throttle. As the boat lunged forward, they both turned and watched the bear amble back into the brush and disappear.

They sped along the east side of the island, heading farther away from its shore and he held her next to him all the way back. The morning sun sparkled on the water, and the thick trees on the island were a deep green against the bright sky, and he couldn't remember ever being happier.

Heading down Maurus Channel of the west side of Meares Island, they could see smoke curling up from a row of houses nestled along the shore to the south of Lone Cone, the small mountain which rose up in a perfect arc of the darkest green.

"That's not Tofino, is it?" Michelle pointed to the houses.

"Tofino's straight across the channel from there. That's the Opitsat Native village."

"I've never actually met an Indian, have you?"

Reid felt her warmth as she nestled next to him. She seemed so sweet, worrying about the bear and talking about Pooh and all those other bears she liked so much, he should probably just tell her. Reid swallowed and drew in his breath. "Well, actually—"

"Oh, Reid, look! Isn't that cute!"

A seal poked his head out of the water just a few feet from

the boat. Like the periscope of a submarine, he swiveled his head around to survey the surface, his big brown eyes standing out like lumps of coal against his slick tan hide.

"There he goes, down under." Reid watched him pop under the ocean.

"What a cutie. I just love seals, don't you?"

"They're pretty neat."

Michelle put her head on his shoulder. "I'm really sleepy. Getting up so early and then all this excitement." She closed her eyes and curled up closer to him.

Reid couldn't tell if she was actually going to sleep, but they didn't talk all the way back. He looked down at her beautiful face, trying to memorize it and wishing they could stay out on the water like that all day. Or forever.

The marina at the resort was quiet as he brought the boat in. The guests were all out fishing and he was glad to see that the *Regina II* was still out as he pulled the skiff into Harvey's slip.

"Michelle," he whispered, "we're here."

Sleepily, she opened her eyes. "I must have really gone to sleep."

"Sure looked like it." He held the side of the dock. "Can you hold us while I get the lines?"

"Okay." She slid over and grabbed the edge of the dock. "Can't be afraid of a few splinters when you're the outdoor type. Me, the outdoor type—what a kick, my friends wouldn't believe it."

Reid finished securing the lines. "Ready?" He held out his hand to help her out.

She took his hand, but then looked around the marina. "Sure is pretty dead down here."

"They're all out fishing."

"Mr. Roessler's boat is still out. He and Dad must not have caught their limit or they'd be back."

"They're probably pretty far out there. I didn't see any of the yachts from the lodge between here and Hope."

"Why don't we just stay here for a while; there's no one

around." Michelle slid over and motioned for him to get back in the boat.

"Okay." Reid climbed in next to her and the next thing he knew she was practically in his lap.

She unfastened the tie that had held her hair back and shook out her hair, letting it fall over her shoulders. He thought it shone in the sun like some precious metal. Then she took off her windbreaker and threw it in the bow on top of the rifle. "Thank you for letting the bear live, Reid," she said softly, lifting her face close to his.

"Think nothing of it." He swallowed hard, then grinned. Michelle's face was there so close to his, it seemed like she wanted him to kiss her. So he did. Then some more. And some more after that.

They stayed in the boat eagerly kissing, tightly fastened in each other's arms, until they heard the engine of the first of the yachts coming into the marina.

"When can I be with you again?" he whispered as she pulled away from him. He felt like he was on fire, that if he even touched the weathered wood of the edge of the dock the whole thing would explode into flames.

Michelle sat up, fluffed up her hair, and grabbed her jacket from under the bow. "Yuk. It's wet." She looked at him. "What did you say?"

"When can I see you again?"

"I'm supposed to have dinner on Mr. Roessler's boat. How 'bout after that. Dinner's usually over by seven."

"Where?"

"Give me a hand, will you?"

"Sure." Reid jumped on the dock and held out his hand for her, thinking that he really should have jumped in the water just to cool off.

She climbed onto the dock and then watched the *Regina II* come past the channel marker, heading for the moorage.

"Where should we meet?" He tried not to sound too demanding.

"Not here."

"I have my own apartment in the employees building."

"That's next to the basketball hoop?" She put on her windbreaker.

"Yeah."

"What number?"

"It's number three, on the ground floor."

"I'll be there at ten." Then she turned and walked quickly down the dock, not looking back.

If the last few hours had been the happiest of Reid's life, the next hours were the longest. He had never felt quite like this before. He could remember craving things in his life, but they were things like pizza, chocolate mocha delight ice cream, tacos, huge warm soft pretzels with lots of salt, Coke, Doritos, and almond brittle from the English Sweet Shop in Victoria. As far as people went, he could also remember wishing more than anything to see the Toronto Blue Jays, to go to a real game and not just see them on TV. He also had a strong wish to meet Wayne Gretzky. But what he felt now was more than a wish. It was a craving. He was craving Michelle Lamont.

How lucky could a guy get! He couldn't believe it. She was actually coming to his apartment! His own apartment all to himself with no one there but him. With his mother miles from there across Clayoquot Sound, safely tucked away in her nice little solar cabin on Palmer's Land.

Reid decided to clean the apartment. As if the Queen were coming, he smiled to himself. He got into high gear and flew through the place picking up dirty laundry, empty food cartons, Coke cans, and dust balls. He stripped the sheets from his bed and used them to bundle up his laundry, then ran down to the laundry room at the end of the complex and dumped the load in the washing machine.

Back in the apartment he swept the rug, getting rid of the twigs and dirt that he'd been tracking in over the last week, realizing that it was getting hard to tell the floor inside from the ground outside.

Next he started in on the dishes. Washing his own dishes

was the last thing he had wanted to do when he finished work each night. All he wanted to do was eat the leftovers he brought back from the kitchen, which meant every single dish in the apartment was dirty. Dirty dishes filled the sink and covered the counters. Why wash them until he'd used up all the clean ones was what he figured.

While he waited for his clothes to dry he tried to do the next geometry assignment for school. Ridiculous. Fat chance. He stared at the book and all he could see was Michelle Lamont. And all he could think about was how it felt to be holding her and kissing her.

Reid took his basketball out to the court and shot some hoops while he waited for the dryer to get done. He stood in the center of the court, facing the basket, holding the ball at his side, then waved at the trees.

Sitting behind the Grizzlies bench tonight is gorgeous Michelle Lamont, famous Vancouver model who is the girlfriend of Reid Dawson. Michelle waves to the crowd and now she's on her feet, cheering wildly at the pregame display of the Dawson Dunk!

Reid messed around on the court shooting hoops until the clothes were done. In the laundry room, he bundled up the laundry from the dryer and took it back to his apartment. He dumped his clothes on the couch and then took his sheets into the bedroom and put them back on the bed.

How experienced was she anyway? He pulled the bottom sheet over the corners and pulled it tight across the mattress. Wasn't this what he had been hoping for and dreaming of, from the first minute he saw her . . . to have her alone in the apartment?

Reid fluffed out the top sheet and laid it carefully over the bed, smoothing it down and tucking in the corners. What if she wanted to and he didn't know what to do? He put the blanket over the sheet and folded about a foot of the top sheet over the blanket before tucking them in. What if he choked? He took the bedspread and covered the bed, then grabbed the pillow-cases. The bed had come with two pillows. He put one case on, then the other. What if she laughed in his face and hit him over the head with a pillow.

Take that, you backwoods twerp! Swat! Thump! She whacks him with the pillow. Just who do you think you are? Inviting me to your apartment when you have all the experience of a grade one moron! It's over you jerk! Whack! Swat! Thump! The pillow breaks open on his head. Feathers fly everywhere. FEATHERS FIT YOU PERFECTLY! YOU CHICKEN-BRAINED CREEP! And she stomps out of his apartment, never to be seen again.

Reid looked at his watch. He still had at least an hour to kill before she was supposed to come to the apartment. Looking at his watch, he realized he'd been on the go since his alarm had gone off at 5:00 that morning. He was too nervous to eat and tired from his cleaning spree. I'll just lay down for a few minutes, he decided. Get my strength up for when she comes.

Reid stretched out on top of the spread and yawned. Within minutes he was asleep. Sound asleep and dreaming. Dreaming of Michelle Lamont.

Chapter Eleven

Reid," Michelle whispered. "Reid? Are you in there?"

Oh Reid, you are so wonderful. I've always wanted to find a guy like you. She lay back in his arms, loving every moment they had spent together.

"Reid." *Knock. Knock.* "It's me." *Knock. Knock.*

I'm glad you don't have a lot of experience. Your passion was so new, so fresh. I love your wild innocence.

Knock. Knock. "Reid?" *Knock. KNOCK. KNOCK.*

Reid sat up in bed. "Oh, man, I've been out cold. She's here!" He leaped off the bed and tore through the apartment to the front door and flung it open.

"I almost gave up on you." Michelle looked worried.

"Sorry. I guess I fell asleep." He tucked in his shirt. "Come on in."

"I can't. That's what I came to tell you." She turned toward the marina. "We're leaving any minute. My dad didn't catch anything so we're going to Barclay Sound."

"You mean, right now?" He was so muddled from being asleep, he wasn't sure what he'd heard.

"Yeah."

"You're leaving?"

"That's what I said." She looked down at the marina again. "Listen, it's been fun."

"Are you coming back?"

"Maybe. My mother's staying in Palm Springs until the end of month so I'll still be at my dad's. It's always possible that we might show up some weekend since he's addicted to fishing. But who knows."

"Can I have your address or your phone number? At least so I can write." Reid ran to the table and ripped a piece of paper out of his notebook. "Here."

"Okay." Michelle scribbled on the paper. "I'll be at my dad's for the next couple of weeks. Then I'm at my mum's. Here's both." She handed it back to him.

"Take it easy, Reid." She seemed to be waiting for something.

Reid shuffled his feet, staring at the paper with her address on it.

"Bye, Reid."

"Bye."

Then she laughed and put her arms around him. She pulled him close to her and kissed him good-bye. In a second she was gone. Running down the path past the lodge.

He stood in the doorway watching her, not taking his eyes away until he saw the top of her head disappear from sight as she went down the steps to the marina. Slowly he closed the door. He slumped back against it and hit it with his fist. Then he was so depressed, he went to the bedroom and climbed back in bed.

Reid didn't wake up until almost noon the next day. Luckily, he wasn't on the schedule for the breakfast shift or he would have missed work. That's all he'd need right now, screwing up work. At least that's one bad thing that didn't happen, he thought, opening the drapes of the living room to be greeted by unrelenting gray and the day's dreary drizzle. The huge trees seemed a dark greenish gray, the sky was the color of steel; even the cedar shakes of the lodge looked gray, and it all matched his mood now that Michelle was gone. It was like she had taken the sun with her.

Getting some school stuff done was the only thing that made sense to him on a day like this. After all, there was nothing better to do and at least he might be able to get a lot of his geometry done before he had to be at work. Reid got out his next assignment, but after few minutes he shut the book in frustration. All he could think about was her. Holding her, kissing her, the way she had begged him not to shoot the bear. He played it over and over in his head, like some incredible movie. The most wonderful day of his life. And it still completely amazed him that a girl like her had actually spent all that time with him, had wanted to stay in the boat the way they had. That she had kissed him good-bye the way she had.

He put the book back on the pile with his other books and got up from the table. He wanted to be in Harvey's skiff again. Reid opened the door and stepped out to get a better look at the water. It was still raining lightly, but there wasn't much wind and the sea looked calm. He was sure there was still gas left, maybe he'd take it out.

When Reid got down to the marina, it was pretty quiet. Most of the boats were out salmon fishing like they had been when he and Michelle were there. As he walked by the slip where the *Regina II* had been moored he felt an aching loneliness. There was no way of knowing if she'd come back with her father. She didn't seem to know whether they would or they wouldn't. Reid watched a pair of ducks, little black-and-white grebes, swimming and diving together near the dock where the huge yacht had been. He couldn't stand the thought that he might never see her again.

By the time he got the tarp off Harvey's boat, the drizzle had let up. He checked the gas. Still a half a tank. Had it just been yesterday morning that she had been sitting next to him as they started out for Hope Island? It seemed like a dream.

Reid drove out of the marina, down the channel past the markers, keeping his speed barely above idle. As soon as he was out of the channel he grabbed the throttle and pushed it full out. The skiff thrust forward and the hull bounced across the ripples in the water and he remembered holding Michelle and how she had looked with the sun on her hair and how she had leaned against him.

Heading north away from Stere, Reid turned the boat toward Hope Island, needing to retrace his ride with her. He saw the speck of the island on the horizon. She had been so excited when she had first sighted it. Then when she begged him for the bear's life, it was totally awesome. What a moment! As he brought the boat in close to the edge of the island, he yelled, "Hey, Smokey, Pooh, Paddington, whoever you were. I wasn't going to shoot you, but thanks for showing up!"

Then he sped off toward Stere. Crossing Father Charles Channel, he saw the smoke curling from the Opitsat village on Meares Island, and he couldn't help remembering what she'd said about never knowing anyone Native. Actually, Indian was what she'd said and he really had been about to tell her, but then the seal popped up and he never got around to it. She had no clue about him being half-Native. What would she think if she knew? Maybe she was the kind of person who wouldn't think much about it one way or the other. After all, there were so many people in Canada who were so many mixtures of backgrounds; seemed like you always heard people saying they were Irish-English-French-one-eighth-Sioux or something like that. Maybe she'd just look at it that way.

But as he brought the boat into the Stere marina, it began to bother him. What a phony. First pretending about this whole bear hunting thing, and letting her believe he might actually have shot that bear if it hadn't been for her. And then her saying she never knew an Indian and here he was, half-Haida. Would she have still liked him if she had known the truth? It began to eat away at him.

He wished he could talk to someone about it. Then it dawned on him that Gloria was coming back to work that afternoon. She'd been easy to talk to until she got all weird before she left. But he was pretty sure she wouldn't still be acting weird, since almost a week had gone by. Being at school and all, she probably forgot about it. He'd talk to her.

Reid was peeling potatoes when Gloria burst into the kitchen. He put the potato peeler down and stared for a second. He'd been so dazzled by Michelle, he had forgotten how pretty she was. She was out of breath and her cheeks were flushed as she fastened her dark hair at the nape of her neck.

"Sorry I'm late, Claude. I tore up from the marina as fast as I could." She caught her breath. "The bus from Ukee took forever."

"No problem. Reid's started on the potatoes. You can prep the lettuce."

"Okay." She grabbed a long white apron and scurried to the walk-in refrigerator.

"Hey, aren't you even going to say 'hi'?" Reid waved the potato peeler.

"Hi," she said flatly and disappeared into the walk-in.

"Sure are friendly today," he mumbled and started peeling again.

Gloria returned with an armful of lettuce. "What's that?"

"I said, sure are friendly today."

Gloria ignored him as she turned on the water and began spraying the lettuce.

"What I'd do to you?" Reid whispered. "I haven't even seen you all week."

Gloria's hands worked quickly, spraying the lettuce, then tearing off the leaves and wrapping them in dishtowels to absorb the moisture. She wouldn't look at him. Reid shrugged and concentrated on the potatoes.

"You missed a spot." Gloria pointed at a potato in the pile next to the sink. "You have to get those dark spots out."

"You're gone a whole week and that's all you have to say?"

Gloria glared at him. "I heard you got involved with Michelle Lamont."

"Who told you that?"

"I just heard." Gloria carried the lettuce back to the walk-in. After a minute she returned to the sink with a colander full of tomatoes. "Don't you know? There are no secrets in a place this small."

"Listen, I really want to talk to you," Reid whispered. "I need some advice."

"So, what's your problem?" Gloria began slicing the tomatoes, not looking at him.

"Not here. Can we talk after work?"

"I suppose so." She paused and held the knife pointed toward him. "Where do you want to talk?"

"If it's not raining, how about the beach?"

"Okay, what if it is?" She started slicing the tomatoes again.

"My apartment?"

"Okay."

The night was still clear when Reid finished work. A three-quarter moon peeked out from behind the clouds, cutting a path of shimmering light across the water. He and Gloria could meet at the beach. He didn't know why, but he thought it would be a lot easier to talk to her out there and not in his apartment. He needed space. It wasn't that easy to ask for advice about this kind of thing, and since Gloria didn't seem to be in the best of moods, it would just be better to be outside.

Curving around a wide inlet, the beach was a two-kilometer expanse on the west side of the island facing the open ocean. Reid ran down the path to the beach, hoping Gloria would wait for him. She had finished work earlier than he had. At the end of the path he made his way across the driftwood logs, huge silver-gray cylinders tossed to the edge of the beach like tooth-picks by the winter storms. The moon was even brighter as he climbed farther out on the logs, and he could clearly see someone sitting on one of them about ten meters to his left.

Reid ran over to her. "Sorry, Claude wanted me to prep a few things for breakfast."

"I just got here a few minutes ago."

Reid sat on the log next to her. "Nice night, isn't it?"

"Beautiful." Gloria grabbed a handful of sand and slowly let it run through her fingers. "It reminds me of one of the prints that Roy Henry Vickers does."

"The Native artist in Tofino?"

"You've seen them. In the beautiful longhouse gallery on Second and Campbell." She grabbed another handful of sand. "He's Tiemshin, from up north near Alaska. He has some prints of totems in the snow. They really knock me out."

Reid picked up a driftwood stick and started poking a pile of rubbery kelp that was tangled in a heap at the end of the log. "I like to step on this sometimes and hear it pop."

Gloria smiled. "Me, too."

"That's the first time you've smiled at me since you got back."

"I guess I was pretty shocked about you and that girl. But walking out here I thought about it and I suppose I shouldn't hold it against her what her father does. Besides," she smiled, "it's hard for me to stay mad at someone."

"She's nice, really." Reid stabbed a piece of kelp. "One time she kept this guy from shooting a bear." He looked out at the ocean, convinced that omitting a few details here was okay, since the main thing was true, and also because Gloria's brother was in that Bear Alert organization and she might think it was wrong even to go on a fake bear hunt. Also, explaining the whole thing was too complicated.

"Look Reid, I'm sure if you like her she's nice."

Reid didn't say anything. The only sound was surf, the waves breaking onto the beach and the popping of the kelp as he poked it. After a while, he stopped poking the kelp and looked over at Gloria. "I feel dumb admitting this, but I've never had a girlfriend."

Gloria pulled the collar of her windbreaker up around her neck. "That's not dumb. Lots of people go all through school and never get involved with anyone."

"I feel pretty out of it, living so long at Heather Mountain." He went back to poking the kelp. Then he turned toward her again. "What about you?"

"What about me?"

"Do you like anybody?"

Gloria slid off the log and leaned back against it. She brought her knees to her chest and wrapped her arms around them. "I sort of did."

"But not anymore?"

"It didn't work out." She rested her chin on her knees and looked out at the ocean. "What advice did you want?"

"It's about being half-Native. Michelle and I passed the Opitsat village and she said that she had never actually known anyone Native."

"She must live in a pretty different world from us. Mars, maybe?"

"Well, you said that's not her fault, right?"

Gloria sighed. "I guess so."

"The problem is that I didn't say anything about being half-Haida. I was about to, but then this seal popped out of the water and she got to talking about seals and it just never came up again. She gave me her address and I want to write her, but I don't know if I should say anything about it."

"Are you ashamed of it?" Gloria's eyes met his.

"No. But I didn't know my dad. I don't even know any Haida people, and the only Native traditions I know about are from the white guys who lived at Happy Children of the Good Earth. It seems so phony."

"When you're mixed you have to be careful about not getting hung up on what race you are. It can make you crazy." Gloria looked up at him and put her hand on his arm. "Listen, Reid. You're who you are. The truth of your life is that your dad was Haida and your mother's white. Maybe you didn't know him or his people, but it's still a fact and nothing can change that."

Reid nodded. Then he smiled. "I was thinking how they said we look like sister and brother. Maybe we're connected, because Native people were supposed to have gotten to North America over the land bridge from Asia."

"Everyone's connected way back somewhere. I don't worry about it much anymore. I think I was in grade nine when I figured out that if anyone had a problem with me being half-Asian and half-white, then I had a problem with them."

The moon shone through the branches, lighting the path that left the beach. Reid glanced at Gloria walking beside him. Her cheekbones were high and smooth, her coppery skin seemed to glow, and her thick, dark hair brushed the top of her shoulders. When she smiled at him, her eyes were midnight black. She was beautiful. He had always thought she was pretty, but tonight there seemed to be something different about her. Or was it him? He wasn't sure. But there was one thing he did know: she was right about what he should do about Michelle. There was no doubt about it. If Michelle had a problem with who he really was, then he would have a problem with her. That was all there was to it. He would write her and tell her the truth.

When they got to the employee building, Reid walked Gloria to her apartment. "I'm going to do what you said."

"I didn't tell you what to do," she protested.

"I didn't mean you were bossy."

"I hope not."

"Anyway, I'm just going to tell her the truth."

"Good luck," she said. "I mean it."

Reid put his arm on her shoulder. "Thanks."

Gloria paused for a moment, looking up at him. "See you tomorrow." Then she turned and went inside, closing the door behind her.

Reid knew he'd never be able to sleep until he had written Michelle. It was a good thing he didn't have to be at work until the lunch shift the next day because he was up most of the night. It turned out to be much harder than he thought. In fact, he couldn't remember ever having written anything harder. He sat at the kitchen table, staring at the walls for hours before he'd even written a word. And when he finally did, everything he wrote seemed stupid. The first letter:

Dear Michelle,
I've been thinking a lot about meeting you. You're the most
wonderful girl I ever met and there's something that I have
to tell you

Smush. He crumpled that one up and flipped it on the floor.
The next one:

Dear Michelle,
How are you doing? I hope you had a great trip back home!
Well, there is a little something I want to tell you

Smush. Crumple. Crunch. And the next:

Dear Michelle,
I sure had a great time with you, but there are a few things
that I didn't get to mention.

Smush. Crumple. Flipped to the floor. Each letter seemed
more pathetic than the last, and by 1:00 A.M. there were a
dozen crumpled sheets of notebook paper lying around the legs
of his chair, looking like he'd dumped over a trash can. He was
no farther along than he was when he started some two hours
earlier.

Reid tore out another sheet from his notebook. Looking at
his books piled on the table made him realize that he'd also have
to tell her that he didn't go to the Mountain Academy. He'd
have to tell her that he went to school on Heather Mountain
with kids from the Happy Children of the Good Earth.

Sometimes he really missed that place. Maybe when you
leave a place you remember the good stuff. He liked how close
everyone was. Although he had to admit, there had been a few
times when the kids didn't get along. Once there had been a
big fight between Rainbow Callanti and Aspen Jones.
Meadow's father made them write letters to each other about
all the things that made them mad. But they had to keep the

letters for a week. Then they could choose if they wanted to give it to the other guy or throw it away. They both decided to throw it away.

Maybe that's what he should do. Write her everything he really wanted to say and then decide later whether or not to send it. Why not? It seemed like it was worth a try. Reid got a fresh piece of paper and began to write. And this time it came easily, it just seemed to flow. Knowing that he might decide not to send it opened him up like he had been uncorked.

Dear Michelle,

I had hoped the last night you were here that I could have talked with you about some assumptions you had made about me that weren't right. I really liked being with you and you seemed to like being with me, but I wanted you to know the truth about me and my background.

First of all, my name is really not legally Reid. My mother is the kind of person you call a hippie or a granola and she named me Moonbeam. Twice we have lived on communes on Vancouver Island. In fact, the only time I lived in a city was about five years in Victoria. My mother is from the States, but her mother is Canadian. She met my father at U.B.C. and he was Native, a Haida. So I am half-Native. Now you know someone who is at least part Native. But I was never raised in the Indian culture. The little I know about it comes from the school we had at the communes where we've lived. This is not the Mountain Academy. We were all home schooled, correspondence kids, with the North Island Regional Correspondence School. I was never on a real basketball team. My father was killed fighting a forest fire in Alberta the summer before I was born. My mother and I left the commune at Heather Mountain (it was called the Happy Children of the Good Earth) a few weeks ago. I got this job at Stere Island Lodge and my mother is living in another commune situation on Palmer's Land outside of Tofino. When I got to Stere I wanted a different name, because I wanted to be more like normal kids. A friend of mine helped me pick the name Reid.

It's for Bill Reid the half-Native (Haida), half-white artist who made the famous Raven and the First Men *sculpture at the museum at U.B.C. (The one that has the little people coming out of the clam shell with the big raven on top.) Now that you know who I really am, I hope you won't have any regrets about being with me when you were at the lodge. And I also hope that you will want to see me again. Because that's what I want more than anything. I hope you'll write me and let me know what you're thinking after you've read this.*

Love,
Reid

Carefully, he folded the letter and then went to bed, sure now that he'd be able to sleep. But no such luck. Over and over again all he could think about was that he hadn't told her that the bear hunt was a fake. Should I tell her that, too? Do I have to tell her everything? Does she need to know that the gun wasn't loaded?

Reid slammed his hand into the pillow and sat up in bed. He just wanted peace of mind but the whole thing seemed to be making him crazier and crazier. He flipped on the light and went back to the living room. He unfolded the letter, reread it, and the added a line at the bottom.

P.S. The first time I actually ever went bear hunting was with you.

He reread the letter three more times and then decided to send it. It'd be the only way he'd ever get sleep again. It was good that the main door of the lodge was always open and the desk clerk was on duty twenty-four hours a day, because by morning he was afraid he might lose his nerve.

Reid threw on his jacket, took the letter, and walked over to the lodge. Frank Hannawalt was at the desk. Reid didn't know him very well; he was one of the newer employees that Jim Goltz had just hired.

Frank was surprised to see Reid come in the lobby. "Are you always up this late?"

"No. I've got an important letter to go out with the mail and I was afraid I'd forget to drop it off tomorrow. The mail boat usually comes while I'm at work."

Frank pulled the mail sack out from under the counter. "I'll stick it in right now. It'll be on its way first thing."

"Thanks. Well, guess I better get some sleep."

"That letter must be pretty important."

Reid looked at the mail sack where Frank had just put his letter and hesitated a minute, knowing if he wanted to, all he had to do was ask for it back.

"It is important," he said quietly, sounding more determined than he felt. Then, before he could change his mind, he crossed the lobby and went out into the dark night.

Chapter Twelve

On Saturday when he wasn't working, Reid crashed at his apartment. He was too tired to worry any more about the letter, totally wiped out from only getting three hours' sleep the night before. By Sunday the letter began to nag at him, but he tried not to think about it. Michelle wouldn't even get it until Monday.

But by Monday, it was all he could think about. He was obsessed with it. What would she think when she first read it? Would she like it? Would it make a difference? Would she be furious with him? Would she hate him? A postcard might come from her right to the lodge, and everybody would know.

Dear Reid Phony Dawson,
In your dreams I'll see you again, you scum.
DON'T write me again! EVER!
  Michelle Lamont

He told Gloria about the letter; it was her spring break and she was working at the lodge all week. When he first told her about it she was really nice, the way she had been at the beach. He kept trying to remember what she had said. "If someone has a problem with who you are, then you have a problem with them." He said it over and over like one of the chants the people at the Happy Children of the Good Earth used to do when they were meditating.

Whenever he got the chance, he'd ask Gloria again if she thought he had done the right thing. "Do you think I'll ever hear from Michelle? Do you think the letter has blown it? Do you think I still have a chance with her?" He couldn't shut up. He was full of so many questions and worries, they popped out of his mouth like he was a suitcase jammed with too much stuff that sprang a hinge.

On Monday she had listened patiently. On Tuesday she had listened. But on Wednesday it was a different story. They had finished work and were walking back to the employee apartments. "What should I do if I don't hear from her? Should I write her again? What do you think?"

"REID DAWSON, WILL YOU SHUT UP!" Gloria yelled at him so loud he almost jumped into the bushes. "You are like a one-way radio that's stuck on send! For three days all I've heard is this garbage about Michelle Lamont and I'm sick and tired of it! Not once, NOT EVEN ONE TIME, have you ever asked me anything about me. Like, How am I doing? What's going on in my life? How was school? Nothing!

"And for your information, I happen to be worrying about something, too. My brother wants me to help him on a project for Bear Alert and it might be a bit risky. And I might have wanted to talk to a friend about it, but no. It's all you, you, you and your stupid problem and at this point I don't give a flying fig what you do! So just bug off. I've had it!"

Reid felt like he'd been flattened by a cement truck. He stood in the path and watched Gloria stomp off to her apartment. She slammed her door so hard, it echoed through the trees, sounding like the building's roof had caved in.

Now he'd really blown it. The one friend he had here, and she would probably never speak to him again. And the worst part of it was, he knew Gloria was right. He had been a crummy friend to her; he couldn't blame her for being so mad at him.

Reid went down to the marina and sat on the dock. Out in the sound, toward the north end of the island, a crab fisherman was hauling in crab traps. He felt like one of those crabs, flailing about, not being able to get anywhere. It felt like he couldn't get anywhere with Michelle, or anywhere without her. What a jerk. He told himself he ought to visit reality. She might never come back here. He should just forget about her. But Reid knew he couldn't. Not until he found out how she reacted to his letter. Until then he felt stuck in neutral, not being able to go one way or the other.

In the distance a Tofino Air float plane flew toward the island. Reid remembered the first time he had seen Michelle when he was substituting for Brad Wellman. She looked like someone from a magazine when she climbed out of the plane . . . *A plane?* He scrambled to his feet as the float plane came in toward the dock. A plane! Why hadn't he thought of it before! Tomorrow was his day off. He could take the plane to Vancouver, see Michelle, come back that same night, and still be at work on Friday. It was perfect! He'd find out for sure, one way or the other, how she felt about him.

Then he realized that it was Wednesday, the day his mother always met with Anne Depue to drop off her weaving at the boutique and hopefully pick up her check if anything had sold. It was like it was meant to be. He could borrow the money for a ticket, then pay her back when he got his first paycheck. Reid left the marina and raced to the lodge to find out what time she'd be there.

Two ladies were in the boutique looking at the clothes when he came in. Anne was talking with one of them. A thin, tan, silver-haired lady whose diamonds were so huge you couldn't help staring. Mrs. Gotrocks. Reid remembered when Abby would see certain women in the lobby of the Empress and whisper, "There goes Mrs. Gotrocks." He thought it was actually the person's name until there were so many Mrs. Gotrocks that he realized his mother gave every rich lady that name.

Anne waved to him and excused herself from Mrs. Gotrocks. "Hi, Reid, did you want to talk to me?"

"I just wondered if you knew what time Mum was coming today."

"She should be here pretty soon." Anne looked at her watch. "She said it'd be late morning, probably around eleven or eleven-thirty. I think she'll really be pleased. I sold quite a few of her things this week." Anne smiled. "I know I am."

"Thanks!"

Reid headed straight for the front desk. This was great! She'd sold some stuff. And not just for her sake, but his, too. She'd probably be in a good mood and very happy to loan him a little money.

Mrs. Shafley, the concierge, was at the front desk. Reid was never sure what hours she worked; her shifts were different from the regular desk clerks. Philline Shafley was different from most people who worked at the lodge. Reid didn't like her. The concierge's job was to cater to the guests and arrange all kinds of things for them and she had an attitude about it. She acted like she was better than the other employees and tried to boss them around. She'd ordered most of the servers from the dining room to bring food to her office. Joani Harr, Helen Paulus, Madalene Lickey, and Sandy Gresko had all been yelled at by her for not bringing it within ten minutes. Even Gloria and Gretchen Coe couldn't stand her, and they found good in almost everybody.

"Mrs. Shafley, I want to fly to Vancouver tomorrow on the earliest flight and then come back as late as I can the same night. How much is the ticket?"

"Must be urgent business." She sounded a bit concerned.

"Not really." *It's none of your business, you nosy old bag.*

Mrs. Shafley leafed through North Vancouver Air's schedule and rate book. "And will you be needing any transportation, car rental, or limousine pickup?"

A limo? Do I look like I'm going to a prom in my jeans without a date?

"No. Just the plane ticket."

"The fare is two hundred seventy dollars for the round trip. That's Canadian."

"I didn't think it would be American," Reid muttered.

"Well, many of our guests don't seem to be able to understand that the world doesn't run on their dollars," Mrs. Shafley said, haughtily.

"Is there anything cheaper?"

"If you book forty-eight hours in advance, the fare is two hundred forty-five." She glanced down at the fare schedule. "And if you book fourteen days in advance, the fare is one hundred and ninety-nine. But since you are in such a hurry to go tomorrow, young man, you don't qualify for any of these discounts." She slammed the fare book shut and gave him a superior smile.

Well, you don't qualify for anything but being a jerk, you puffed-up cow.

"Would you like to purchase a ticket?" she asked sweetly.

Reid looked out at the trees through the bay windows at the end of the lobby. He had never spent his life thinking about money or wishing he were rich. But at that moment, there was nothing he would have liked more than to have had a huge wad of one-hundred-dollar bills stuffed in his pocket, which he would casually pull out. Slowly he would peel off one bill, then another right under her needle nose, right in her face. Take that, you fat goose. And that. And that. He'd buy every seat on the friggin' plane. She would faint. Then she'd get fired for lying down on the job.

Reid looked back at Mrs. Shafley. "I have to think about it. Maybe I'll come back later."

He walked through the lobby and saw that Mrs. Gotrocks was still in the shop. Maybe she'd buy some of his mum's stuff, every last jacket and shawl Mum had woven would be snapped up and then when he asked her for the loan, she wouldn't even blink. *Of course, I can loan you this money, honey. Take even more because after all you'll need to eat something when you're in Vancouver and you'll need a little for bus fare. Just pay me back when you can, I know you're good for it. No problem. Have fun!*

Two hundred seventy dollars. That was a lot of money. He had no idea just an hour's plane ride would cost that much. What a shock. Reid started calculating his wages. A week's pay came to three hundred seventy-two dollars. And he'd probably need at least ten or fifteen more to spend when he was there. Four and a half days of work in a steaming kitchen peeling potatoes and washing dishes to spend a few hours with Michelle.

Michelle. He said her name to himself. Michelle. He had never met anyone like Michelle Lamont. Someone that beautiful. Someone who lived in Vancouver and rode around in yachts and planes. Someone who had kissed him. Someone who had wanted to come to his room. Reid sighed, remembering kissing her in Harvey's skiff. Too bad she had to leave that night. What would have happened if she had stayed? Reid sighed again. He had to find out how she felt now. Even if it did take four and a half days of scrubbing pans and peeling potatoes, it would be worth it to see her. He had to. That was all there was to it.

It was a little after 11:00 when Harvey and Abby arrived at the lodge. Reid had been waiting at the slip where Harvey moored his boat, and he grabbed the line from the bow as Harvey eased the old boat in next to the pier.

"Hi, Harvey. Hi, Mum. Anne's got good news."

"Really?" Abby threw him the line from the stern. "You've talked to her?"

"A little while ago. I don't know how much is sold, but she was real happy about it."

"Gee, everything's turning up roses." She jumped on the dock and hugged him. "Have you missed me?"

"Sure. Want me to carry your stuff up to the shop?" Reid looked at the boxes piled neatly in the cabin.

Harvey joined them on the dock. "I think she wants to wait until she sees how much more Anne might want."

So now you're the big expert on Mum.

Reid glared at Harvey, but in a second he felt a little sheepish. Harvey had been nice to him. It was just hard to get used to having the guy in the picture.

"Mum, there's something I have to talk to you about."

"Okay, we can talk on the way to the shop." Abby linked her arm through Harvey's.

"Well, I'd rather talk alone."

Harvey looked at her. "That's fine, I can just wait on the boat."

"Harvey, you don't have to." She held his arm.

Yes he does. Get on the boat, dude.

Harvey climbed over the rail and waved them on. "Go ahead." Then he disappeared into the cabin.

"Moonbeam, you—"

"I'm not—" He interrupted, then stopped himself.

"You're not what?"

"Nothing."

"Look, I just want you to recognize that Harvey is important to me and that—"

"Duh."

"What's that supposed to mean?"

"Duh. Like you think I'm stupid. That I haven't noticed."

Abby walked up the steps. Reid didn't say anything as he followed her. He'd gotten off on the wrong foot, getting bent out of shape about Harvey. It just bugged him sometimes the way the guy had moved in on her. He wasn't a bad guy. Probably a pretty decent guy. What set him off was how she expected him to not even blink. Just welcome the guy with open arms like they'd known him for a hundred years. Saying that stuff about recognizing that Harvey was important to her! Like he was always supposed to recognize what was important to *her.* Like living on Palmer's Land, for instance. What about what was important to *him* for a change? Did she ever think about what *he* needed? Reid decided he better stop thinking this way. He'd have to chill out if he hoped to get anywhere with her about the loan.

At the top of the stairs Abby pointed to the bench on the bluff. "I suppose we can talk over there."

"I'd rather go to my apartment. It's more private."

"Okay. If you say so." Abby followed him down the path. "It's still hard for me to believe that you live somewhere by yourself."

"I wouldn't be, if you wanted a job here."

Chill. Be nice. Don't blow it. Maybe actually needing something from her was what was getting him so uptight, Reid thought as they walked toward the employee apartments. It had been a long time since he had asked her for anything. He couldn't remember how long. She was always the one asking him for help.

They didn't say another word until they reached the apartment. Reid opened the door and she went in after him. For a minute Abby just stood in the middle of the living room, like she didn't know how to act.

"Have a seat, Mum."

"Oh. Okay." She sat in the chair across from the couch. "So, do you like it here?"

"It's great."

"Have you been keeping up with your school work?"

"Pretty well."

"That's good." Abby looked at the pile of books on the table. "So what did you want to talk about?"

"I need to borrow some money."

"What about the money you make here?" Abby scowled, looking confused.

"I don't get paid until next week, after I've been here two weeks."

"Well, how much do you want to borrow?"

"Two hundred seventy dollars, and I'll pay you back next week as soon as I get paid."

"Moonbeam!"

"Aggh." *I hate that stupid name!*

"What in the world do you need that kind of money for?"

"Why does it matter, since I'm going to pay it back?" He stood up and went to the kitchen and got himself a Coke. "Want something?"

"No thanks," she snapped. "It matters because I'm still your mother. How do I know it's not for drugs or something!"

"Gimme a break."

"I'm serious. I'm not participating in something I don't even know about."

"Okay, okay." Reid tried not to sound as exasperated as he felt. "It's for a plane fare."

"Where? Don't you have to work?"

"I'm going to Vancouver and back on Thursday. It's my day off."

"It's to see that girl, isn't it?"

"So what." Reid drank his Coke, swallowing it in large gulps. "How do you know about her anyway? Did Harvey say something?"

"No, he didn't. I saw Gretchen Coe in town and she mentioned it."

"What a bunch of busybodies around this place. I can't believe it." He took another swig of the Coke.

"There usually aren't many secrets in a place this small."

"Where have I heard that before?" he mumbled.

"What?"

"Nothing. So can I borrow the money or not?"

"I think you're making a big mistake. And I'm not just saying this because of what her father does for a living."

"Good. Because it's not her fault."

"Believe me, I know girls like that. I grew up with them. They're materialistic and superficial and you're going to get hurt. She can dabble in your world, but you don't belong in hers. You can't believe how snotty she was in Anne's shop. Gretchen told me that's who it was that day." Abby stuck her nose in the air, impersonating a snob. "My mother *only* buys Missoni."

"You can't judge someone from one little thing like that."

"I can't stand her type and I know it well. You just met her. You don't really know anything about her."

Reid smashed the empty Coke can. "You're one to talk! You get involved with this Harvey guy and you hardly know him! You just jumped right into it!"

Abby stared at him. Then she stood up and went for the door. "Fine. If you think the decisions I make at age thirty-five are the equivalent of what you do at fifteen, then there's nothing else to say." Then she walked out.

"Fifteen and a half!" he shouted at the door as it closed behind her.

Oh great. Now she's mad, too. What a mess. Reid picked up the Coke can and threw it in the trash. Why did it matter to her who he liked? It was his life. She could do what she wanted with her life and he was going to do what he wanted with his. He didn't care what any of them thought. There was no way he would give up trying to see Michelle.

He knew he could always wait until he got his paycheck and then just buy a ticket for his day off next week. But the more he thought about that, the more next Thursday seemed really far away. Like a year. Hey. Maybe all he had to do was ask Jim Goltz for an advance on his pay. Why not? After all, he was supposed to get his check on Monday anyway. And it wasn't like he was asking for money he hadn't earned. He could even ask for a check to cover the days he had worked so far and then just get the rest of what was coming to him on payday. It was worth a try.

He didn't see his mother again. He didn't want to try and find her. He had too much pride. He thought about hanging around the lobby or down at the marina to maybe just bump into her. But he was too proud for even a lame attempt like that. And he knew she had been too mad to try and find him because she left early that afternoon without saying good-bye. But after the dinner shift, when he came back to his apartment, he found a note on his door.

Dear Moonbeam,
Too much has changed too fast. Let's be like the United Na-
tions and at least keep talking. I'll be back next Wednesday.

Love,
Mum

P.S. Anne asked me how you got your nickname. I just
said that I didn't know because I didn't know what she was
talking about. Do you?

Reid put the note on the table with his books. He'd probably have to tell about his name. He knew she'd be really upset,
but he should probably take the hit and get it over with. Then
maybe in a few weeks this would all have blown over and he
and Mum would actually be able to talk to each other without
fighting for a change. He hoped so; he didn't like it when they
weren't getting along. He glanced at the note again, and then
went to take a shower. He thought it would be best not to be
all pitted out and stinking like a gymnasium when he went to
ask the boss for an advance.

Jim was in the office when he got there. Reid was glad he
didn't have to go looking for him all over the lodge, he might
have lost his nerve.

"Got a minute?" Reid stuck his head in the doorway.

"Sure. Just going over the books." Jim swung his chair
around away from the computer and motioned to the chair
across from the desk. "Have a seat."

"Thanks." Reid looked around the office. Had it really only
just been a few weeks since he and his mother were here, when
he applied for the job? She was right. A lot had changed, and
it had been fast.

"Wait just a second while I finish this." Jim turned back to
the computer, entered something, and then swiveled around
to face Reid. "Now, what can I do for you?"

"I was wondering if I could have an advance on my pay-check. Or at least the part I've earned so far?"

Jim leaned back in his chair. "It's our usual policy not to do that. It just messes up the books, and believe me, they're hard enough as it is. But payday's Monday. Is there some kind of emergency?"

"No. I just wanted to go to Vancouver for my day off to-morrow and need plane fare."

"You don't have to buy a ticket." Jim smiled.

"Huh?"

"The lodge reserves seats all season on Wickaninnish Air Charters. It's a service we provide for guests. If all the seats aren't taken we let the employees fill them."

"You're kidding?" Reid couldn't believe the good news.

"We don't make a big thing of it, since the guests have pri-ority. But all you do is go down to the marina at eleven A.M. when the first flight leaves. If there's an empty seat, you can get on."

"Really? That's great, but what about the return?"

"Those are booked in advance for guests arriving through Vancouver. I can check and see how it looks." Jim turned back to his computer and brought up a different file. "Looks like there's a threesome that will be picked up at six and that will leave a vacant seat, unless of course one of the guests wants to take that seat in the morning. But unless that happens, you're in luck. You'd just have to be sure to be at the plane by six."

Reid thanked Jim several times before he left the office, not quite able to believe the great deal that might just possibly have fallen in his lap. Now, if only all the guests would cooperate. But that was out of his hands, so the only thing he needed to decide now was whether or not to call her to say he might be coming. He could probably reach her if he called early, before she left for school. But what if she told him not to come? What if she said she was busy? Then he'd never know if she really did have plans or if it was just an excuse and she didn't want to see him. If he just showed up and surprised her, he could tell from how she reacted if she was happy to see him. A person couldn't fake their feelings that easily when you surprised them. Then he'd know once and for all how things stood between them after the letter.

To call or not to call. He went back and forth about it all evening and finally around midnight came to a decision. Not to call. He'd just take his chances that he'd find her home after school. Or find out where she was if she hadn't gone straight home. He didn't want to risk a phone call.

Thursday morning Brad Wellman waited for the plane with Reid. It was almost 11:00 when they heard its engine, and at 11:00 sharp Joe Martin waved from the cockpit as he brought it in for a landing. Brad and Reid helped secure the plane and then Brad opened the door for the two passengers who got out, rich-looking business guys loaded with fishing gear.

Reid held his breath, turning back to the lodge, hoping no one else was coming. Maybe he'd make it. The two men left the dock, followed by Brad, loaded down with their gear.

Joe climbed out of the cockpit and stretched his legs. "Nice morning. Wish I could get a little fishing in." He stretched his arms and then checked his watch. "But I've got to turn around in about five minutes. This stop isn't much more than a touch and go."

"I'm hoping to catch a ride with you," Reid explained. "It's my day off. Thought I'd spend some time in Vancouver, then come back with you at six."

"Doesn't look like anyone else is going. Wait here while I check at the front desk." Joe smiled. "If there aren't any other passengers, you're on."

While he waited for Joe, a large yacht sailed into the marina. Reid watched it come slowly toward the dock. It was huge. Sparkling white with gleaming brass and mahogany, it looked like the *Regina II*. The waves from the yacht washed against the dock and Harvey's skiff rocked back and forth as they rolled under its narrow hull. Reid gazed at the skiff, remembering the deserted marina the afternoon they came back from Hope Island, being alone with her when nobody was around. Just the two of them alone in that skiff.

"All set!" Joe yelled. He gave Reid a thumbs-up from the top of the marina steps. "It's a go."

"All right!" Reid slapped the piling next to the plane. Then he opened the door to the Cessna and climbed in. It was happening. Luck was with him once more. In a few hours he would see her.

Chapter Thirteen

Reid took the slip of paper out of his pocket and rechecked the address. The last thing he needed would be to get lost trying to find the place. It had already been confusing enough just getting the bus out here from Coal Harbour, where the plane had come in.

He loved every minute of the flight from Stere Island. Reid had only flown one other time in his life, to the States to visit his mother's family. That was it. They'd never gone back again after that. He was only about a year old and didn't remember it anyway. But this flight was really something. It was incredible how they could be on this west coast wilderness with its miles of isolated sandy beaches, migrating whales, and colonies of sea lions and in just an hour come down to glass-and-steel skyscrapers and a city of over a million people.

Reid walked along Southwest Marine Drive and stopped near the Marine Drive Golf Club to check the map he had gotten in the bus station. He was pretty sure he was supposed to turn right, and then it looked like Laurel was two blocks east of that. He put the map back in his pocket and crossed with the light.

He had never seen such big houses. They looked like museums. Why did people need all that room? It wasn't like they had such big families. Michelle only had her half sister, Ashley, and that was when she was living at her mother's house, not her father's. She was the only kid when she was there. Maybe he should have called after all. Shaunassey was one of the wealthiest neighborhoods in Vancouver, and he felt like he had landed on another planet. Most of the garages were three times the size of their cabin on Heather Mountain. And the yards were the size of soccer fields, with manicured gardens and flowering shrubs and fruit trees. Every mansion seemed to have rhododendrons as part of the landscaping, so huge their blossoms looked like basketballs. At first he wasn't sure where to look for the house numbers. Then he noticed them on gates that ran across the wide driveways, or etched in stone pillars carved like lions or some kind of creature. Some would be on a plaque set in a stone wall that enclosed the whole property.

He turned on Laurel Drive. Her street. This was it. His hands shook a little as he checked the address and began looking for house numbers. In the middle of the block was a huge English Tudor mansion. The wrought-iron gate was open and Reid stopped in the foot of the driveway and checked the address again, 24012 Laurel Drive. Not that he didn't have it memorized, but he wanted to check again, just to be sure. No mistake about it. This was it. A large circular driveway curved from the street to the front door and back out to the street. A green Ford pickup was parked in the drive. Cautiously, Reid started up the driveway and went to the truck and read the lettering on the door. USHIBA'S LAWN AND GARDEN SERVICE.

An Asian guy was clipping the edge of a lawn so perfect it looked like a putting green. Reid went over to him, feeling more like he was walking across a skating rink in slippery leather shoes than across an asphalt drive wearing sneakers.

Reid cleared his throat. "Hi, um, excuse me."

"Yes?"

"I'm a friend of Michelle Lamont's and wondered if she's home."

"I just work outside. Ask the housekeeper." He motioned to the front door.

"Okay, thanks."

Well, at least he knew for sure this was the right house. Michelle hadn't given him a phony address or anything like that. So she must have really wanted for them to stay in touch, he tried to convince himself as he rang the bell.

After a few seconds another Asian person appeared, a middle-aged woman dressed in a crisp pearl gray uniform. She looked like she could be related to Gloria, he thought. Or even him since he and Gloria were supposed to look something alike.

"I'm Reid Dawson. Is Michelle home? I'm a friend of hers from Stere Island Lodge."

"Is she expecting you?" From her accent, Reid thought she might be Chinese. He could see into the huge entryway with its marble tile and dark mahogany beams. He'd never seen a place like it except the Empress Hotel, or something in a movie. But never anyone's real house.

"Well, no, not exactly." Reid showed her the slip of paper with Michelle's writing. "But she gave me her address."

The woman nodded. "She'll be home from school any minute, then she go to ride."

"Can I just wait out here?"

"Outside, yes. That be fine." She closed the door, like she was relieved that he hadn't asked to come in.

Reid leaned against one of the pillars, watching the street for a sign of Michelle. The yard guy had finished and was putting his equipment in the pickup. Reid looked out over the manicured lawn and the elegant landscaping. Michelle's house seemed about as far away from Heather Mountain as you could get. He had trouble believing he was actually here.

But she did give me her real address, he kept telling himself again while he watched the street. She could have made something up. Or just told him to forget it, but she didn't. And she was the one to make the move to kiss him good-bye, and in the boat, too. Maybe when she saw him she'd invite him to go for that ride the housekeeper said she was going to take after school. Maybe she would. Maybe she had some errands to run or something. And afterwards they could go to Stanley Park and stop in some secluded spot.

Oh, Reid, I've dreamed of being with you again, like we were in the boat. Seeing you again so soon is the most wonderful surprise. Let's make the most of every moment.

Reid was closing his eyes, imagining being with her in the secluded spot at Stanley Park, when he heard a car. The gate automatically opened and a shiny black Land Rover drove in, swung around the drive, and pulled up at the front entrance. Michelle jumped out of the driver's seat. There was an athletic-looking blond girl on the passenger's side in the front and another girl in the back, pretty, with light brown curly hair. It looked like they were each wearing navy blue sweaters with some kind of crest on the pocket. He used to see kids in school uniforms in Victoria sometimes, kids who went to private schools. But he never pictured Michelle wearing a school uniform. He had only imagined her in jeans and casual stuff like she had worn at the lodge, that she would look the same, and everything would be the same.

Michelle ran around the car jingling her car keys and then stopped in her tracks. "What are you doing here?"

"Hi," Reid smiled nervously, "thought I'd surprise you."

"How wonderful," she said, sarcastically.

"Hey, Chelle," the blonde called, as she put down the window: "What have you been hiding from us?"

The back window came down. "Who's your friend, Chelle?"

Michelle's face got red and she mumbled, "This is Reid Dawson. Listen, um, Reid, we've got to get to the—"

"Aren't you even going to introduce us?" the girl yelled from the back seat.

"Oh all right," Michelle sighed. "This is Reid Dawson. This is Megan," she motioned to the front seat, "and Daria in the back."

"*The* Reid Dawson!" Megan shrieked. "Your little spring break thing!"

"At least you picked a cute one." Daria giggled.

"You guys shut up." Michelle glared at them. "Listen, Reid.

We've got to be at the stable in twenty minutes, and I've got to change, then take Megan and Daria home to change before we get there. So I've really got to run."

"You don't even have a few minutes?" Reid jammed his hands in his pockets and rocked back and forth on his heels.

"You're cold, Chelle," Megan teased. "You don't even have time to offer him a nice bowl of Wheaties, the breakfast of champion hunters!"

Daria cracked up. "Wheaties? We prefer granola, don't we, Chelle!"

"I told you two to shut up," Michelle whined. "Reid, I've got to go, I'm sorry." She unlocked the front door and disappeared into the house.

Reid looked at the ground, wishing he could evaporate. Who else had she showed his letter to? The whole bloody school? He wanted to run. Don't give them the satisfaction. Don't run like a scared rabbit. As much as he wanted to, he wouldn't give them that. He was going to walk out of there past those two witches like they were nothing to him. They were just noise. He focused his eyes on a tall cedar across the street. Not taking his eyes off it, he slowly walked down the steps and across the driveway.

"Hey, Reid, we liked the name Moonbeam a lot better!"

He could hear them laughing and shrieking all the way to the end of the drive, but he kept his pace steady and slow, steady and slow. *If someone has a problem with who you are, then you have a problem with them.* He said it over and over, trying to block out their giggles and shrieks.

Then they started to sing. "Mummy wants me for a mooooooonbeam, a moooooonbeam—" singing at the top of their lungs.

He didn't run until he got to the end of the block. Then he took off as though he were fleeing some kind of noxious gas. Some invisible chemical that would destroy him unless he got away in just seconds. He ran all the way to the bus stop. *If some-one has a problem with who you are, then you have a problem with them.* Problem? He wasn't sure what he felt more: a humiliation so deep it pierced through him like a javelin, or rage. How incredible that people could be hurt and humiliated and not fight back. His mother had preached nonviolence his whole life and he didn't realize until this very moment what it took to try and live that way. If he had a loaded gun right now, he could actually imagine going back there and blowing them all to pieces.

At the bus stop he waited, catching his breath, then he took out the bus schedule and looked at his watch. He had a few hours to kill before he had to be back at Coal Harbour to get the plane. There must be something he could do that would keep this trip from being total poison.

He pulled the Vancouver map out of his pocket and noticed that on the back it had a list of points of interest. His hands shook as he held it. The Vancouver Aquarium . . . Gastown . . . the Capilano Suspension Bridge. He couldn't go to them all. Reid thought about each place, trying to make the best choice. Maybe he should go to the aquarium, he thought, imagining being there. Then he imagined Michelle being there.

TEENAGE GIRL KILLED BY WHALE
AT AQUARIUM

Michelle Lamont, 16, of Vancouver was killed today when Moonbeam, a magnificent Orca whale, accidentally dove from his tank, crushing Ms. Lamont. Other bystanders, friends of Ms. Lamont, were maimed for life in the freak accident.

Or maybe Gastown, the oldest section of Vancouver. Maybe that's where he should go. He couldn't visualize that point of interest without seeing her there, too.

GASTOWN STATUE BLAMED FOR
DEATH OF GIRLS

The famous statue of Gassy Jack, Vancouver's first saloon keeper, toppled today in a freak accident, crushing to death Michelle La-

mont, 16, of Vancouver. Other bystanders, friends of Ms. Lamont were also killed. Their identities have not yet been released
pending notification of next of kin.

There sure was a lot of stuff to do. The Capilano Suspension
Bridge was cool. Another tourist attraction where she would
show up.

BRIDGE SNAPS SENDING TEENAGE GIRL
TO HER DEATH

The Capilano Suspension Bridge, spanning the canyon 70 meters above the Capilano River, snapped today as extraordinary
turbulence, a rare atmospheric phenomenon known as the
Moonbeam Gust, appeared without warning, destroying the
bridge and hurling Michelle Lamont, 16, of Vancouver to her
death on the rocks below. Several unidentified friends of Ms. Lamont also on the bridge at the time of the mishap, remain in
critical condition.

Reid continued to study the points of interest on the back
of the map, imagining Michelle's death at each one, an activ-
ity which gave him considerable satisfaction. Then he looked
over the list of museums, seeing her crushed in freak accidents
as various sculptures and paintings fell on her head, and finally
decided to go to the U.B.C. Museum of Anthropology. That's
where Bill Reid's famous sculpture was, and it made him think
of the day Gloria had helped him figure out his name. That day
had been a good day.

It looked like it was a straight shot out to U.B.C. on the
bus that ran along Southwest Marine Drive. The only thing that
worried him was that he had seen something called the South-
lands Riding Club on the map and figured that was probably
where Michelle and her friends were going. He didn't think he
could stand it if they drove by in their Land Rover and saw him
waiting for the bus; drove by laughing their heads off, singing
"Mummy Wants Me for a Moonbeam."

She can dabble in your world, but you don't belong in hers. His mother's words came back to him. He hated to admit that she had been right. For the past few years she had leaned on him for everything, always asking his advice, and he just never thought of her as someone whose judgment he could trust. But he also knew that even if he had a suspicion his mother might be right about Michelle, nothing would have stopped him from getting involved with her. There are some things you have to find out for yourself, no matter what people tell you. Especially your mother.

On the bus to U.B.C., Reid looked out at the broad streets. The cherry trees were almost through blooming, and their fallen petals clung to the curb like soft pink confetti. The houses were smaller than the mansions in Michelle's neighborhood. But they were still monstrous compared to where he had lived most his life: small apartments and one-room cabins. Where *did* he belong? Even living in these smaller houses with their tidy rectangular lots would be like suffocating. All the cars, the exhaust from the buses. He wanted to be back on the west coast of Vancouver Island. He knew that much.

But he couldn't see living at Stere Island Lodge forever either, and being home schooled. He'd had it with that. But living with his mother in that small cabin on Palmer's Land was out of the question. They'd drive each other crazy. It was too small. The past two weeks they hadn't gotten along very well, and they weren't even living together. Reid got that feeling again when there was too much to think about, like his brain was scrambled. He was glad when he arrived at U.B.C.

At the museum he stopped in the gift shop near the entrance and got a small brochure and map of the museum. The gift shop had fancy books; some were the same as ones in the lodge, but then he noticed one the lodge didn't have. An entire book about Bill Reid. The cover was a deep rich brown with a photograph of a stunning gold carved box with a bird on the top. The title in gold lettering simply said *Bill Reid,* with the name of the author, Doris Shadbolt, at the bottom in smaller letters. Reid picked up the book and scanned the jacket flap.

> . . . *a visual artist of monumental power and highest accomplishment . . . Born in 1920 to a German-Scots-American father and a Haida mother, Reid grew up in British Columbia.*

Reid looked at the price of the book. He had to have it. He pulled out his wallet and checked his money. He'd only have a dollar left once he'd bought it, but he already had his bus ticket back to Coal Harbour. And he didn't need to buy food; after seeing Michelle and her friends, he'd lost his appetite. He went to the register and bought it.

He spent almost a half-hour looking at the huge cedar sculpture, *The Raven and the First Men*. It was a famous sculpture, and although it wasn't the first time he'd seen it, it felt like the first time. He was blown away by it. The only person he'd ever heard of who had one parent who was a Haida Indian and the other who was not only white but an American who then became a Canadian—was this guy who had made this incredible thing!

As Reid circled the sculpture, an older man who looked Native came in the room with a group of students. Some of them were taking notes, and the man, who wore glasses and was dressed in a sport coat, seemed to be in the middle of giving a lecture. "Bill Reid was in his early teens before he even became conscious of the fact that he was anything other than an average Caucasian North American," he stated in a deep voice.

Reid's ears perked up and he inched a little closer to the group.

"Bill's quest to learn about his heritage probably began with the natural curiosity of most teenagers to know where they came from. In his case, since he had no knowledge of his father's relatives, he became interested in his mother's family."

Reid watched closely as the man moved next to the sculpture and pointed to the raven. "His grandmother belonged by birth to the Raven clan and his family crest was the Wolf."

The man giving the talk waited while the group walked around the sculpture. Reid thought he was probably on the museum staff, or maybe a teacher at U.B.C. He really wanted to talk to him since he seemed to be an expert on Bill Reid, but he couldn't quite get up the nerve. He felt like he'd blown every bit of nerve he had on this stupid trip to see that witch.

Instead, he decided to hang around and listen, but after a few minutes the man led the group to another room. Reid felt a little silly following them, but he did anyway, careful to stay a few paces behind.

"This sculpture, *Carved Cedar Bear,* is inspired by the myth that tells how the Bear clan was established. In the story of the Bear Mother and her Husband, for instance . . ."

Reid's mind drifted away as he stared at the magnificent bear carved by Bill Reid. He thought about his ridiculous bear hunt with that rich witch and it made him wince. But the more he looked at the extraordinary sculpture of the huge bear, the more he began to feel a kind of powerful energy contained within the smooth cedar surface. His mother had said you could feel the hand of the Maker on wood sometimes. Is that what she meant? He didn't know, but it seemed that something inside him was beginning to settle down just by sitting near the bear and looking at its smooth limbs, the huge claws, the large dark eyes.

The group of students and their teacher left for another room, but Reid stayed behind, mesmerized by the bear. He stayed for about twenty minutes and then took one last look at *The Raven and the First Men* before leaving the museum.

On the bus Reid pored over his new book and found a description of Bill Reid that seemed to speak directly to him. ". . . there is obviously a part of him that longs for the warmth and security of the extended family community . . . so his awakening awareness had to do with family, for he was as yet unacquainted in any conscious way with the whole body of Haida culture or art."

Reid closed the book and looked out the window at the rows of well-kept houses with their beautifully landscaped yards and he realized how much he missed the only extended family he had known, the people at the Happy Children of the Good Earth. People he had lived with for five years, one-third of his life. It wasn't that he wanted to live that way again. It was too small for him, now. But recognizing he'd never go back to it made him sad.

When he got back to Stere Island, Reid headed for the beach. He was in no mood to talk to anyone, and looking at the ocean always made him feel better. He sat on the driftwood log where he had been with Gloria and looked out at the dark storm clouds forming on the horizon. The wind had picked up and the waves crashed as they broke on the beach. *How could he have been so stupid?* But then he wondered, if Michelle had been happy to see him, would he ever have found out what she was really like? He watched wave after wave break across the sand, and it began to dawn on him. If his letter hadn't made any difference, if she didn't care that he was half-Native and didn't go to a private school and was from such a different background from hers, then she would be someone he could really care about.

He picked up a fistful of sand and let it run through his fingers. He was the one who had dumped her! Maybe he hadn't told her off, but he had dumped her from his mind. She'd never know it, but she was history. He found out what she was really like and he didn't want any part of her!

He jumped up and ran toward the ocean, then picked up a rock that was embedded in the wet sand and hurled it into the surf. It was like throwing her away, and he threw one rock after another, each one farther out than the next. Stretching himself as the wind whipped against him and the salt spray stung his face.

He leaned down to get another rock, then turned in surprise. Gloria was running across the sand, calling to him.

"Didn't you hear me?" she said, breathlessly. "I've been looking all over for you!"

"I didn't hear a thing. The waves make so much noise."

"Reid, your mother's been arrested—"

"Arrested! For what?"

"Bear Alert disrupted a hunting operation run by a guy named Orville Webb. The RCMPs were called and the people in the Bear Alert boat were charged with harassment. Your mum was in the boat . . . so was my brother."

"Where is she now?"

"She's in the town jail in Tofino and Harvey is—"

"Jail! Isn't there a fine or bail or something?"

"Harvey's offered to help, but she's not sure what she wants to do until she talks to you. Harvey came back to get you."

"What about your brother?" Reid asked as he hurried with her across the beach.

"He's okay. He's out on bail," Gloria told him, slightly out of breath as they ran along the path. "I was involved, too, as one of the lookouts at Grice Bay, so I didn't get arrested. But your mother is really gutsy."

Reid waved to Harvey from the top of the marina steps, then hesitated for a minute. "I should have been helping you guys instead of going to Vancouver." He looked away, embarrassed. "She was a real witch. I suppose you knew all along."

"When a girl who looks like that throws herself at a guy, he's a sitting duck."

"I know I've been a really lame friend. I'm sorry."

"You better go," she said quietly, catching her breath.

"You're not still mad?"

Gloria didn't say anything for a minute. Then she smiled.

Reid didn't know what to say. "I better get down there." He returned her smile, feeling grateful. "Is there anything you need in town?"

"No. I'll see you when you get back." As he left, she called after him. "And tell your mother I'm behind her all the way!"

It began to rain. A number of yachts were slowly coming through the channel to the marina and Reid could see a group of people scurrying to break down the gear of a huge sailboat at the end of the dock where Harvey moored his boat.

"Glad Gloria found you. I must have just missed you." Harvey grabbed the line and pulled it in, holding it as Reid climbed over the rail.

"I was at the beach. How's Mum?"

Harvey looked upset. "She doesn't seem to want to listen to anything I have to say right now. She only wants to talk to you."

"I'm her family." Reid's eyes met Harvey's with a steady gaze.

Harvey nodded, then he started the engine as Reid got the lines and pulled in the bumpers. As they got underway, the sky got darker and it began to pour. There was rough weather ahead.

Chapter Fourteen

There were only two cells in the Tofino jail. Small, grim spaces, they were walled on three sides with concrete blocks, with bars and a barred door enclosing the front. Each one was furnished with two steel beds, a stainless steel toilet, and sink. The first cell was empty. Abby sat on the steel bed in the other, waving jauntily when she saw Reid. Upbeat, cheerful, trying to give him the impression that everything was perfectly fine. But he knew better. Her eyes were scared.

"Hi, Moonbeam," she chirped as Thorin Olson, the guard, let him in the cell.

"Sorry about this," Thorin apologized. "It's the rules."

"We understand." Abby smiled graciously as he shut the door, locking them both in.

"Jeez, Mum. All I do is leave the area for one day, and—"

"No lectures, honey."

Reid sat next to her on the bed. He looked around the sparse cell, taking in the cold concrete blocks, the sink, and toilet without so much as a wall for privacy. It was quite a price for her principles. "Guess you've lived in better places, eh?"

"I don't think the Queen's coming." She smiled, hoping he'd joke with her.

"Probably not." He tried to return her smile, but it was a weak attempt. "Look, I don't get this. I just don't really understand why you're in jail. Harvey explained the charges to me, we're not talking about a big crime here. Don't you just pay a fine and that's it?"

"Bear Alert educates people to bring an end to trophy hunting and the trade in bear body parts."

"I know that, Mum," Reid said quietly, trying to be patient. "I don't need the speech."

"When we intercepted Orville Webb and his slimy California customers, I know we sent a message to him that his drive-by beach shootings aren't going to be so easy." Abby scooted back on the bed and crossed her legs under her. "I can't believe people think that's a sport. Driving a boat next to the shore, jumping out on the beach downwind of a defenseless animal, and gunning it down!"

"I know, Mum."

"They're organizing in the states, too. There's a group in Michigan, called C.U.B., Citizens United for Bears, that's trying to get a petition to change their laws. Can you believe it's legal there to set out bait to train the bears to feed in a certain spot? They put out pizza and doughnuts and all kinds of junk, then the hunters go to where the bears come to feed and shoot them at point-blank range."

"That's terrible. But Mum—"

"And hunting with dogs is legal there, too. They put radio transmitters in the dogs' collars. The dogs chase the terrified bear for hours until it's exhausted and climbs a tree. Then the so-called hunters go to the place where the signal comes from and shoot the bear out of the tree. This has to stop all over North America!"

"Mum, forget the speech, okay?" He looked at the bars of the cell. "Please?"

"Okay."

"Why are you the one in jail? Just tell me that."

Abby sighed and finally explained what had happened. Four of them had been arrested: Gloria's brother, John Burgess, Gretchen Coe, Art Lockwood, and Abby. A number of other people had been involved, but only as lookouts to alert them if Orville Webb was in the area. After John Burgess was arrested he decided to pay the fine. He would be back at U.B.C. in the fall when the judge from Port would be in Tofino for the trial. He decided staying in the Asian communities working to stop the demand for bear body parts was a better use of his time than coming for the trial. The other two, Gretchen and Art, wanted to go to trial to bring the issue to the attention of the media. They each had lawyers, a woman and a man from Vancouver who represented the logging protesters without charge and wanted to help Bear Alert. Abby explained that each defendant was required to have a lawyer and there weren't any other lawyers in the area who would represent her without charge. "And Bear Alert is against using taxpayer's money for public defenders," she added.

"It seems pretty obvious what you should do, Mum. Just pay the fine and leave these beautiful surroundings."

"Harvey says he'll pay for one of the top lawyers in Vancouver if I want him to. He makes it all so easy."

"Harvey must have a lot of money."

"He does."

"I thought you didn't like rich people."

"Not all rich people. There's just a certain type I can't stand, and Harvey's not that type."

"So what's the problem?" Reid stood up. "Just tell the constable that you won't pay the fine and then go to trial."

"It's just that I'm afraid of being too dependent on Harvey. You know I'm a romantic person. I believe in love at first sight, but you have to be careful. Sometimes it turns out to be lust at first sight."

"I found that out."

Abby sat forward. "Things didn't go so well with that girl?"

Reid walked across the small cell and leaned against the wall facing her. He hated to give her the satisfaction of telling her she'd been right. And he didn't like having been so stupid. But at least he knew she wouldn't rub his nose in it; his mum could be flaky, but she wasn't mean. So after a minute he just told her. "She was like you said."

"I'm sorry, honey." Abby anxiously twisted a strand of her hair around her finger. "Are you okay?"

"Sure. But I did a lot of thinking while I was there. And I know I can't go back to the way we used to live. I want to go to school in Ucluelet next year. And there's something I've got to tell you. It's about my name."

"Your name?"

"I changed my name. Ever since I've been at Stere Island Lodge I've—"

"What's wrong with your name? Moonbeam Dawson is a perfectly good name!"

"It's weird."

There was a long silence. Finally she said, quietly, "Okay. I admit it's unusual. But it's a beautiful name. It's a cultural thing, Moonbeam. Take for instance a name like Red Feather, that might sound weird for someone of Irish descent or French or something, but if you're Native it's not weird at all."

"But Moonbeam isn't even a real Native name. You just made it up!"

"That never bothered you before, Moonbeam."

"My new name is Reid. It's from Bill Reid the Native artist who's half-white and half-Haida."

"Really?" she seemed to soften a little. "How'd you happen to think of that?"

"Gloria helped me figure it out."

"Oh."

"I changed my name on my application form at the resort. And I wrote the NIRCS about it and told them to change it on all my records."

"Just like that! Behind my back! Why didn't you discuss it with me, Moonbeam?"

"Reid. Start calling me Reid, Mum. Everybody at work does."

"Look, I have to sign permission forms for you to be in correspondence school, I'm still your parent. You can't just go do these things!"

"I didn't say you weren't."

"This is too much. First you eat meat, then you change your name—" her voice started to break.

"Mum, I know this isn't easy. But I'm going to find out what I have to do to make it legal. I might have to wait until I'm eighteen or something, but in the meantime, it's Reid whether it's legal or not."

There was another long silence. Abby ran her hand through her hair and looked away from him, shutting him out. "I don't know if I'll be able to remember not to call you Moonbeam," she finally said, her voice so quiet he could hardly hear her.

"You can if you put your mind to it." Reid tried to cheer her up. "Gloria said you were one gutsy lady."

Abby couldn't help smiling.

"See, Mum, I just want to be more like regular kids."

"That's what you mean about going to Ukee next year, I suppose."

"Yeah."

"Well, I know there's an easy solution. Harvey wants me to live with him, and there'd be plenty of room for the three of us. I don't think you'd feel cramped there." Abby bit her lower lip. "He's serious. I mean, he says he's at a place in his life where he wants marriage and kids. But I have to establish myself here, I don't want to just cave in and let some man take care of me. And who knows if we really are right for each other?" Abby twisted her hair tight around her finger. "You understand, don't you? It takes time. I mean after all, we just met! Don't you think I'm right?"

"I can't tell you, Mum. It's up to you."

"Do you like him?"

"He's come on pretty fast. But I think he's a good guy."

"Maybe we could add on to the cabin on Palmer's Land. A whole separate room for you. What do you think about that idea?"

"I think we better get you out of jail first. One way or another." She looked so pathetic sitting on the bed in the cell. It was a familiar feeling. Worrying about her, feeling sorry for her. But he'd been doing a lot less of that since Harvey had been in the picture. "Mum, if Harvey did pay for your lawyer and then it turned out that you wanted to break up, would you feel obligated to stay with him?"

"No. I'd feel bad, but not obligated."

"Then I think you should let him help."

Harvey was pleased when Reid called him from the jail to let him know Abby would take him up on his offer. Not only pleased, but grateful. "I hated seeing her in jail, even if it wasn't for that long," he confided, his voice flooded with relief.

It was odd, having Harvey feel grateful to him. But it felt good, more equal somehow. Within twenty minutes of Reid's call, Harvey had paid Abby's bail and taken her to Palmer's Land. A man of action, Reid had to admit. His mum could use that.

Reid stayed at Harvey's that night after calling Jim Goltz, who arranged with Claude to have Reid work the lunch and dinner shifts the next day, instead of the breakfast and lunch shifts that had been scheduled. It had been a long, exhausting day, and Reid went to bed as soon as they got to Harvey's after they dropped Abby off at Palmer's Land.

In the morning, there was a steady drizzle as Reid and Harvey boarded the Clayoquot Biosphere Project boat. The seagulls, ever optimistic, flew around the old fishing boat hoping some morsel might find its way into the water as they left the dock and headed out from town to Duffin Pass.

"I was north of here up at Baseball Bay when Abby was arrested," Harvey said as he steered around Felice Island. "I wasn't an official lookout for Bear Alert since the biosphere project is strictly scientific. But since I happened to be up there anyway for the project, John Burgess asked me to radio them if I saw Orville Webb, which I did. Guess I have to admit it bothers me sometimes that I'm not on the front lines, so to speak.

You know, the way Abby has been. That she was the one to get arrested."

"Don't feel bad. I think she was doing the part she wanted to do." Reid laughed. "I'm surprised Mum didn't run on shore and throw herself in front of the bear to protect it."

Harvey chuckled and glanced at Reid, and they exchanged smiles of mutual understanding.

"Want to take it?" Harvey offered the wheel as they moved past the southern tip of Stubbs.

"Sure." Reid changed places with him and took over. He steered first a little to the port side, then starboard, getting the feel of the boat. "It handles pretty well."

"For an old tub."

"How far have you taken it?" Reid asked.

"Prince Rupert is about as far north as I've gone."

"Been up to the Charlottes?"

"Haven't yet, but hope to someday. There's a project called Sandspit 2006 going on in the Queen Charlotte Islands/Haida Gwaii. They use both the Canadian and the Native name. Anyway, they're in the midst of a community-based economic planning process. Logging's been their mainstay and now they want to diversify and stabilize their economic base. I've thought about doing some consulting for them."

"That's where my dad was from."

"Do you have any relatives there?"

"Probably. But the impression I got from Mum was that my dad's family had a lot of problems. He was the only one to make it and they resented him. Supposedly, they broke off ties with him when he went to university." Reid looked over at Harvey. "But who knows? Maybe he broke it off with them."

Harvey hesitated. "Ever think you'd like to go up there someday?"

"I don't think Mum would want to." Reid carefully turned the boat, rolling over the waves, cutting down the angle of the pitch of the boat.

"I was thinking about just you and me going up."

Reid let the wheel move through his hands, angling over

the next wave. "I'd like to do that, someday." Then he smiled, and pointed the bow straight for Stere.

It was a hot day in the middle of July when they got word that the judge from Port would be in Tofino in October for the bear trial. Abby told Reid about it on her weekly visit to meet with Anne Depue. It was the peak of the season at the lodge and Abby's designs had been enormously successful. In fact, she had trouble keeping up with the demand, not a problem she had ever been faced with before.

Reid was down at the marina helping his mother and Harvey unload her boxes for the shop when a huge yacht came slowly toward the dock, heading straight for the slip next to them. Reid looked up, squinting in the hot summer sun. It was the *Regina II.*

Michelle Lamont spotted him from the deck and began madly waving. "Hi, Reid!" She wore khaki shorts and a bright orange halter top and Reid couldn't help but laugh to himself, remembering what Gloria had said about his not having had a chance.

Harvey took the last box from Reid. "Abby and I can take these up. We'll see you at lunch."

Abby lifted several of the boxes, which were stacked in a pile on the dock. "Right. You shouldn't have to work on your day off." She walked down the dock with Harvey. "We'll see you in the dining room about one," she called over her shoulder. "Our treat!"

As soon as Abby and Harvey were at the end of the dock, Michelle climbed down from the yacht and made a beeline for Reid. She smiled, tossing her hair back as she leaned close to him. "How are things going?"

"Okay," he said casually.

"Didn't I just overhear that it was your day off?" Her voice was seductive, breathy and soft.

"That's right."

"How 'bout taking me out for a ride in your boat? Or maybe we could go to the beach?"

"I've got other plans."

"Oh." Michelle seemed genuinely surprised. "Well, maybe later. We'll be here for about three days."

"I'm busy." Reid said matter-of-factly. Then he smiled and left.

As he walked away from the marina, he realized that even though he still didn't know exactly who he was or exactly where he belonged, he did know what he was not: a boy toy for Michelle Lamont.

When he was at the top of the steps, Gloria called to him from the bench on the bluff, a spot where she often sat and read before work. He waved and headed to the path that ran along the bluff.

The breeze picked up and the leaves on the huckleberry and salmonberry bushes on the edge of the path rustled. If the wind got stronger there might be some good surf. One of these days he was going to learn, that was all there was to it, Reid thought as he watched whitecaps forming on the water. He got to the bench and sat down next to her.

"Good book?"

"Very. Margaret Atwood's latest." Gloria closed the book. "Was that who I thought it was?"

"Yeah. She wanted me to take her out in the boat."

"Are you going to?" Gloria asked, trying to sound non-chalant.

"I'm only a sitting duck once." Reid smiled and slipped his arm around her. "I told her I had other plans."

"What plans?"

"I said, 'I have to cut my toenails.' "

"You didn't really say that!"

"No, I wish I had. But I'm always thinking of stuff I wish I'd said when it's too late." Reid smiled at her. "But I do have something important to do this week. The lawyer that's representing Mum in the bear trial is also going to file papers for me to change my name legally. I'm going in town to sign them tomorrow."

"So it's official." Gloria looked up at him. "That's great."

"Did I ever really tell you . . ." he hesitated.

"Tell me what?"

"How much it meant. That you helped me get the right name?"

"I knew you liked it."

"I hope so." Reid looked into her dark eyes, so similar to his own. He felt connected to her, and it wasn't like they were brother and sister. He wanted to stay next to her.

The warmth of the July sun enfolded them and above, the huge cedar boughs swayed as the summer wind came off the ocean. And he wanted to kiss her.

Maybe someday, Reid thought, as he left to meet Harvey and his mother at the lodge.

About the Author

Jean Davies Okimoto is a widely published author of children's and young adult books, including *Take a Chance, Gramps!*, *Molly by Any Other Name*, and *Jason's Women*. She is the recipient of the American Library Association "Best Books for Young Adults" Award, the IRA/CBC Young Adults' Choice Award, the Parents' Choice Award, the Washington Governor's Writers Award, and the 1993 Maxwell Medallion for Best Children's Book of the Year. Two of her books have been recognized as *Smithsonian* Notable Books. Her work has been translated into Japanese, Chinese, and Italian, and has been adapted for television for *Bedtime Stories* on HBO and Showtime. Her play *Uncle Hideki,* based on her novel *Talent Night,* was produced at the Northwest Asian-American Theatre, and her plays for young people have been produced in New York, Toronto, and Vancouver.

She and her husband, Joe, have four grown children, three grandchildren, and two dogs. They live in Seattle and are frequent visitors to British Columbia.

.